THE OUTLAW TRAIL

DAKOTA CHASE

EVIL PLOT BUNNY LLC

THE OUTLAW TRAIL

Repeating History Series, Book Five

An imprint of Evil Plot Bunny, LLC

PO Box 722

Loughman, FL 33837

Copyright Ó 2021 by Dakota Chase

Cover by Alexandria Corza

Published with permission

ISBN 978-1-951777-30-2

www.evilplotbunny.com

First Printing: February 2021

Printed in the USA

PROLOGUE

Winter officially came to the Stanton School for Boys in the form of a Nor'easter, a screaming storm of howling winds and a belly full of heavy snow. The snow blew in sideways and coated everything—the quad, the buildings, the sidewalks, and anyone unfortunate enough to be outside in it—with a thick coat of freezing white flakes. There was already a good foot of fresh powder on the ground and at least another twelve to fifteen inches predicted before the storm blew itself out. Waist-high drifts nestled against the buildings and trees surrounding the quad.

Ash's teeth chattered, and he pulled his coat collar higher up on his neck. He tugged his hat down lower over his ears, which felt like twin blocks of ice attached to the sides of his head. His sneakers did nothing to protect his feet from the cold, and his toes were already numb. From the knees down, his jeans were soaked and well on their way to freezing solid. "I'm just asking why he can't ever tell us to come see him when it isn't monsooning outside." He had to practically yell to be heard above the whistling wind.

Grant huffed, his white puff of warm breath lost in the

snowstorm. "This is a blizzard. Monsoons are rainstorms, genius."

"Snow is water, just colder. Same difference."

"You're an idiot."

"What I am is frozen, and I may never thaw out. You can point to me and tell people 'Here's my boyfriend, Ash. He used to be alive, but now he's a fucking ice sculpture.'"

"Since when are you my boyfriend?"

Ash grinned, even though the cold made his teeth ache. "Since you stuck your tongue down my throat the other night and tried to lick my spleen."

Grant made a rude noise that Ash knew he didn't mean. "God, you make everything sound so sexy. Seriously, you are a total romantic."

"Was that sarcasm? I think that was sarcasm."

"Wow. Like I said, pure genius."

Ash jabbed a good-natured elbow into Grant's side, then decided it was too cold to fool around. He shoved his hands deeper into his pockets, lowered his head, and hurried on, anxious to reach the classroom building and get inside out of the storm where he could melt in relative warmth. When he finally reached the building, to show Grant he cared, he didn't even let the door slam shut in Grant's face, instead propping it open with his foot.

Unfortunately, since it was the Christmas holidays, the building's heat had been lowered, keeping it only warm enough so the water pipes wouldn't freeze and burst. In other words, while it was warmer than being in the storm outside, it wasn't exactly toasty, and Ash's chances of completely thawing out were relatively slim.

He did begin to melt a little, though, trailing drops of water on the linoleum floor in his wake. He took off his wet hat and shoved it into his pocket, hoping his ears would defrost and not crack off the sides of his head.

They headed upstairs, to where Mr. Ambrosius's history class was located. Ambrosius, known to the two of them as Merlin, was their history teacher and one of the world's most powerful wizards. The first part of his resumé was known to everyone at the school; the second half was a secret known solely to Ash and Grant, and then only due to a series of unfortunate events.

Ash and Grant had both been in trouble with the law and been on their third strike when they happened to be scheduled to appear before the same judge, the Honorable James Fredrick of Eastman County. As a result, they'd caught a break and been offered the choice to either attend the Stanton School for Boys, a structured, disciplined, almost militaristic high school, or be sentenced to a juvenile detention work farm. Not surprisingly, since neither was keen on spending their senior year digging up potatoes or milking cows or doing whatever the hell juvies on farms did, they'd both jumped at the first option.

Which is how they found themselves assigned as roommates in the dorm at Stanton's and in Mr. Ambrosius's history class together.

Neither Ash nor Grant liked each other at first glance. Ash thought Grant was a stuck-up, rich butthead who'd never had to want or work for anything in his life but had everything handed to him on a platter.

Ash knew Grant thought he was a trashy, two-bit criminal who wouldn't know good taste or manners if they crept up and bit him on his ass.

They butted heads almost immediately and continued their feud in Mr. Ambrosius's history class. He banished them from the classroom and sent them to his office to await whatever punishment he deemed appropriate for their outburst.

Which, unfortunately, was like locking two lit matches

3

inside a room full of dynamite. They soon began to argue again and, when their fight escalated into a physical altercation, accidentally ignited a fire. They escaped unharmed, but Mr. Ambrosius's office, including his collection irreplaceable historical artifacts, was destroyed.

Ash and Grant found themselves facing the real possibility of being charged as adults with counts of arson and destruction of property, and would've been sentenced to prison if not for Mr. Ambrosius's rather unorthodox offer.

Turns out, Mr. Ambrosius's first name was Merlin, as in the one-and-only-Camelot-King-Arthur-and-the-Round-Table wizard, and he had a plan for the boys to redeem themselves. Instead of having them arrested, he would send them back in time to retrieve each of the articles they'd destroyed. After all, if Ash and Grant went to prison, Merlin would still be missing his precious collection. This way, he had a shot at getting it back and the pleasure of torturing Ash and Grant often and with great gusto, like today, summoning them to the classroom during the worst storm of the year. At least, that was Ash's take on Merlin's motives. Merlin himself had never enlightened them on the subject.

Of course, at the time Ash and Grant thought Ambrosius was nuttier than Aunt Martha's holiday fruit cake, but agreed it would be in their best interest to accept his offer rather than spend the next ten to fifteen years of their lives locked away in prison. They figured they'd just play along with whatever psycho role-playing game Ambrosius had in mind, and be done with it.

Except Ambrosius wasn't crazy and proved it when he sent the boys back in time to ancient Egypt to retrieve a pendant known as the Eye of Ra from King Tutankhamen.

Since then, Ambrosius had called them in on weekends and holidays—naturally, they wouldn't be lucky enough to miss class because of a time-travel field trip—to send them back to different time periods with instructions to retrieve one of the objects destroyed in the fire.

Today was no exception. While the rest of the school's population had gone home to their families for holiday meals, gifts, and hours of carefree video gaming, Ash and Grant were stuck at the school, braving what might turn out to be the storm of the century in order to get to the classroom so Ambrosius could send them back in time yet again.

All things considered, even with the freezing cold and bitter snow, and despite all of their complaining, Ash knew it was still miles better than being in prison.

At least, that's what Ash told himself, but it was really hard making himself believe it when his feet felt like size-eleven ice cubes.

They took the stairs in tandem, running up quickly, as if the exercise might warm them. All it did was produce a sweat, which quickly chilled under their wet coats. Halfway down the upstairs hall, they skidded to a stop and stared at the door of the history classroom.

"Where do you think it'll be this time?" Grant chewed his lower lip and shuffled his feet, obviously stalling for time.

"I have no idea, but I hope it'll be someplace warm." Ash was happy to dawdle right along with Grant. A puddle formed under their feet as the snow melted off their clothing.

"Oh, yeah. A nice island in the Caribbean. Aruba, maybe, or Bermuda." Grant sighed and smiled. "I could really go for a swim in that warm, turquoise water."

Ash figured Grant, coming from a rich family, had prob-ably been to both, hence the dreamy sort of smile on his face, and felt a stab of jealousy. He'd never been south of the Mason-Dixon line. "I'd settle for a nice beach in Florida."

"Yeah? Where? South Beach?" Grant grinned at him. "I

haven't been there since I was a kid. I remember the white sand."

Ash didn't want to admit the only beaches he'd ever seen were the ones in New Jersey. Instead, he gestured toward the door. "No sense in prolonging the inevitable, huh? You know how he gets when we keep him waiting."

Grant sighed and nodded. "Yeah. Might as well." He reached out and knocked, then pulled the door open. They hurried inside and walked up to the front where Merlin's desk dominated the room.

Neither of them was surprised the room was empty. It wouldn't be the first time they beat Merlin to the classroom —although he would never, ever agree with their assessment. He didn't deviate from routine this time, either.

"Late, as usual." Merlin's voice, deep and strong and completely at odds with his elderly appearance, reached them. Neither of them were surprised they hadn't heard him come up behind them—considering how dry he looked, they doubted he'd braved the storm to get there. Most likely, he'd magically popped in.

He stood in front of the now-closed door, a scarecrow-thin man dressed in a tweed jacket with leather elbow patches, a pair of neatly pressed khaki pants, and a gray button-down shirt. A polka-dot bowtie completed his outfit.

Ash doubted Merlin even owned a pair of jeans. He'd never seen Merlin dressed in anything other than what he and Grant called "Ye Olde Tyme Professor Couture." He often got the impression Merlin would only be more comfortable if dressed in a wizard's robe and pointy hat.

Merlin sported a beard, and while it was long, it was neatly trimmed and relatively free of food particles. At the moment, his face, wreathed in wrinkles and as leathery as an old shoe, was wearing a frown, as it usually did. In fact, neither he nor Grant could remember Merlin ever smiling, although they had seen a spark of amusement twinkle in his blue eyes from time to time.

They knew from experience not to argue with him. "Yes, sir. The weather is really nasty outside."

"Indeed." Merlin strode to his desk and took his seat behind it. He turned toward the window, where outside, the snow continued to swirl. The quad wasn't even visible—the view was a solid curtain of white. "This is nothing. I've seen storms where the snow was so deep one couldn't dig oneself out until the spring thaw."

Ash no longer had any doubt about anything Merlin claimed to have experienced. Merlin was several hundred years old and a powerful wizard. If he said this wasn't much of a storm, well then, it wasn't. Not that the information made Ash any warmer or dryer.

Grant spoke up, obviously anxious to get going. "What are we going to look for this time, Mr. Ambrosius?" They both knew better than to call him the more familiar "Merlin" to his face. He would consider it disrespecting their elder, and nobody in their right mind disrespected Merlin, not if they didn't want to find themselves with a lightning bolt shot up their ass.

Merlin turned back to them and arched a bushy white eyebrow. "In a hurry to leave my company?"

"Oh, um, no, sir. Not at all." Grant paled a little, and Ash braced himself for a possible lightning strike.

Luckily, Merlin didn't seem to take offense. "Very well, be that as it may." He opened his desk drawer and withdrew a piece of paper. After placing it on the desk, he slid it toward Ash and Grant.

Ash peered at the image on the paper. It was a copy of an obviously very old black-and-white photograph of a young man. His hair was messy, and his face, while open and friendly-looking, sported a slight smirk.

"This is a copy of a tintype. Do you know what that is?" Merlin glanced at Ash, then at Grant.

Ash offered the obvious answer. "A photograph?"

Merlin snorted out a breath. "Quite correct, Mr. Uh. One of the very earliest sorts. The name comes from the process —images were processed on thin sheets of metal instead of glass. It made photography less expensive and faster, allowing photographers to produce an image in ten to fifteen minutes instead of hours. This particular tintype represents someone very special to me. I owned something that once belonged to this man, which you two destroyed in the fire."

Ash cringed. "Mr. Uh" was the nickname Merlin had saddled him with on his very first day at the school. He'd been asked a question, to which he'd replied, "Uh..." Merlin seemed to think it was funny. There was just no figuring on what a centuries-old magician would find amusing.

"Who is it in the photo, er, tintype?" Grant wanted to know.

"The leader of a group of outlaws called the Wild Bunch." Amusement glinted in Merlin's eyes. "At the time, they were the most infamous outlaws in the American West. The man in this tintype?" He pointed one long gnarled finger at the paper. "Is Butch Cassidy. This is actually his mug shot from an arrest in 1894."

"Butch Cassidy, as in Butch Cassidy and the Sundance Kid? Seriously?" Ash's eyes popped open wide. "Holy sh... cow. They robbed banks, right?"

Merlin shot Ash a piercing glare for his near-use of a curse word. That would've garnered a lightning strike for sure. "Among other things. Banks. Trains. Stagecoaches, so on and so forth."

Grant huffed. "He doesn't look very wild to me."

Ash turned to Grant and gave him a slight push. "Dude! You've never heard of the Wild Bunch? The Hole in the Wall

Gang? They were like the greatest bank robbers of the Wild West!"

"Jeez, I never realized you were a Wild West geek." Grant smirked, which made Ash want to deck him. Then kiss him. Then deck him again.

He settled for nudging Grant again, a teensy bit harder this time. "What's the matter? You never played cowboys when you were a kid?"

Grant nudged him back. More like shoved, actually. "My folks took us to a dude ranch one year. Does that count?"

"Dude ranch?" Ash snorted. "Do I want to know what that is?"

"Not what you're thinking, asshat. It's a ranch where city people go to be cowboys for a week. They ride horses, cook on campfires, learn to use a lasso, that sort of thing."

Ash smiled, albeit grudgingly. "Oh. Huh. That actually sounds kind of fun."

Grant grimaced. "Fun? I got poison oak, nearly got gored by a bull, and there was a rattlesnake in the outhouse. And I didn't eat beans again for a year afterward."

"Ouch." Ash smothered a laugh under a fake cough. "Okay, then."

"As delightful as this conversation has been, might I return your attention to the matter at hand?" Merlin tapped the paper on his desk with obvious impatience. "You will go to the year 1899, where you will seek out the Wild Bunch and procure Butch Cassidy's gun."

Grant gaped at Merlin. "His gun! Mr. Ambrosius, an outlaw like Butch Cassidy isn't going to let a pair of teenagers just walk off with his weapon. It's impossible!"

Ash nodded. "He'd kill us first!"

Merlin smirked at them. "Then I would suggest you use stealth when procuring it."

"How will we even know it's the right gun?" Grant looked

as nervous as Ash felt. Going into the past to steal the gun of one of the most famous outlaws of all time seemed like the absolute worst idea ever.

"Finally, an intelligent question!" Merlin offered a dry chuckle. "It is a Colt .45, a single action army revolver. Most telling, it will have a series of numbers scratched inside the gun's right grip. Twenty-two, fourteen, eight, and two hundred thirteen. No one is certain what the numbers mean, but many think they're the combination to a safe. If so, it hasn't been found."

Ash's eyes popped open wide. "Whoa, you mean there might be treasure?"

"I am not interested in the may-or-may-not-be valuable contents of a might-or-might-not-exist safe. I am only concerned with getting my property back, which in this case, is Mr. Cassidy's Colt .45, which you destroyed. Originally, Mr. Cassidy turned his weapons over to the sheriff hoping to get amnesty after a train robbery in 1899. In fact, the gun became known as the Amnesty Colt. I was able to procure it through an auction many years later. Unfortunately, since you two dunderheads destroyed it, you'll need to steal it before it's ever turned over to the sheriff."

"What makes you think he still has it?" Ash shrugged. "I would think outlaws had more than one gun in their careers, right?"

"He'll have it because I say he'll have it. He was fond of it, thought it was lucky for him, and used it for most of his career. Any more questions?" Merlin scowled at Ash. Thunder rumbled inside the classroom, a sure sign of Merlin's displeasure.

Ash knew better than to persist. Some things Merlin said needed to be taken on faith, and besides, Ash was not keen to have a lightning bolt zapped up his rear end any time soon. "No, sir. None at all."

"Good. Then off with you." Merlin waggled his fingers in their direction.

Lights began to flash inside the classroom, and Ash barely had time to glance at Grant before a familiar feeling of vertigo twisted his stomach as everything started to spin wildly. Mercifully, before he could puke up the stale Pop-Tart he'd wolfed down for breakfast, it all went dark.

CHAPTER 1

When the darkness lifted and he'd allowed an extra minute or two for his head to clear, Grant took stock. He found himself lying flat on the ground with the taste of dusty earth in his mouth. He turned his head and spat it out, then slowly sat up. A few drops of water hit him in the face. It was starting to rain.

Perfect.

He tried to assess the situation they were in. Both were dressed in pants—not jeans, at least not the kind he or Ash had ever worn but made from some sort of wool material. There was no zipper—only a folded fly with a button to keep it closed, and they were held up by a pair of cloth-and-leather suspenders. They wore off-white shirts made from a rough material, clumsily stitched and loosely fit. Their pants and shirts had obviously been through some hard wear and multiple washings, judging from the faded color and signs of mending. Both boys also had a brightly colored cotton kerchief tied around his neck. Ash's was red, Grant's was blue. They wore calf-high leather boots on their feet, and their heads were protected by brown wide-brimmed felt hats with high, round crowns.

Ash was also stirring and spitting out a mouthful of sandy dirt. He sat up and arched his back, groaning at the audible crack his spine made. "Seriously, can't he *ever* dump us gently? I always feel like I've been run over by a bus when he sends us back."

Grant shrugged. "I don't know. Maybe it's the way the magic works."

"Yeah, or maybe he's a malachite."

"I think you mean masochist. Malachite is a rock."

Ash wiped a sleeve over his face. "Tomato, to-mah-to. It's starting to rain, but at least it's not cold and snowy. How come it's not winter here?"

"Beats me. I know we're in 1899. That's the year Merlin said he was sending us, but he neglected to tell us *when* in 1899 we'd be. Not winter, for sure. I also have no idea *where* we are." Grant stood up and stretched. He braced his hands on his hips and looked around. "Well, one thing's for sure. We're not in New York. Or Chicago, or any other city I know. From the looks of the area, we could be in either of the Dakotas, Wisconsin, Montana, Wyoming, Oklahoma, Idaho, Utah…practically any state west of the Mississippi and east of the Pacific."

Ash eyed him from boots to hat and back again. "Well, wherever we are, you look adorbs, Woody."

"Who?"

"Woody. The cowboy from *Toy Story*. Come on, you had to have seen it as a kid."

He huffed. "I remember the movie. I do not look like a cartoon character."

"All I said was you look adorbs."

"Stop saying 'adorbs.'"

"Why? It's fitting."

"Ass."

"You gonna start that again?" Ash grinned at him. "Come on, tell me I don't look hot as a cowboy."

"You don't look hot as a cowboy." The lie stung his tongue, but he managed not to crack a smile. For about ten seconds. "Okay, sure. You look hot. And I, evidently, look like an animated Tom Hanks."

"You look ador—"

Grant held up his hand. "Don't say it." To change the subject, he turned and purposely looked over the vista spread out in front of them.

They were standing on a high bluff of orangey-brown rock. Behind them, white-tipped mountains soared to touch the sky; below them, miles of hard country stretched. Wide plains covered with an undulating blanket of golden grass rolled out in every direction in a practically unbroken vista. He squinted and spotted a tiny town in the distance, squatting on the plain like an ugly gray mole on a flat, hairy, beige hide.

Grant gestured toward the town. "Merlin always drops us near or at where we should be. Guess that's where we should head."

"Yeah, and we need to find Butch Cassidy. Maybe he's there, or at least somebody in town might know where he is. We'll just mosey on down and ask."

"Are you insane? In case you didn't realize it, Butch Cassidy is a criminal. A wanted man. We start throwing his name around and one of two things is going to happen. Either they're going to think we're criminals, too, and jail us —or hang us, depending on what they think we did—or Cassidy is going hear about it and think we're bounty hunters or something and shoot us."

Ash rolled his eyes and snorted. "You've been watching

too many old movies. Anyway, we *have* to ask. How else are we going to find him?"

"All I'm saying is we need to be careful." Grant picked his way down the bluff, his feet skidding on scree more than once. It was raining harder now, and he was glad for the wide-brimmed hat that kept his line of sight relatively clear. "We have to be smart."

"I'm plenty smart."

"Then prove it. When we get to town, we need to blend in and keep our ears open. If we have to speak to anyone, let me do the talking."

"Who died and crowned you king of the cowboys?"

Grant huffed, slipped again, and nearly fell, but managed to right himself at the last moment. "Just do us both a favor and keep your trap shut, okay?"

"Whatever you say, your majesty." Ash tripped over a root and his feet flew out from under him. He landed on his butt and skidded down a few feet. "Shit!"

"You okay?"

"Yeah. Just dented my pride. And my butt. Why did Merlin give us high-heeled boots? Are we putting on a drag show with Butch Cassidy?"

Grant snorted and reached out to help Ash to his feet. "All cowboy boots have heels like these so their feet won't slip out of the stirrups."

"Truth?"

"Yup. And they have pointed toes so they can slip into the stirrups easier too. Also, boots help protect their ankles against snakebite."

"How do you know all that?"

"Dude ranch, remember?"

"Oh, yeah, that's right. Rich kid. Well, what do you know? Learn something new every day." Ash grabbed his hand and let Grant pull him up. Instead of letting go, he pulled Grant in and stole a quick kiss.

"Hey, what's that for?"

"Every time you get to be a rich boy know-it-all, I get a kiss. It's a thing."

"It is not!"

"It is now." Ash grinned.

Grant scowled at Ash and nearly gave in to the impulse to shove him back down on his butt, if not for the fact that Ash was a really, really good kisser and looked absolutely hot as a cowboy. Not that Grant was going to admit it. Not a chance. Instead, he swallowed his smile, turned around, and began picking his way down the bluff again.

Ash stopped him. "Hey, wait a minute. How come Merlin sent us back to get a gun, without giving us any of our own? Aren't cowboys supposed to have guns?" He pantomimed drawing a revolver from a holster and shooting it from the hip. "We should be able to protect ourselves."

Grant spared Ash an exasperated glance. "Do you know how to load a gun? Shoot it? Clean it?"

"No."

"Well, there's your answer. Neither do I. We'd probably shoot ourselves in the foot sooner than hit a target. Merlin is old, but he's not stupid."

"I guess. Still, how are we supposed to fit in with people like Butch Cassidy if we're not armed? What kind of outlaw doesn't have a gun?"

"Our kind. Now, come on. I want to get down there to the town before we drown out here. It's coming down harder now, and footing is difficult enough without adding mud to the equation. I don't want to break a leg out here and end up as dinner for a pack of wolves or a hungry bear."

"See? If we had guns, we could protect ourselves."

"Again, I remind you neither of us knows how to shoot."

17

"What's to know? You point the business end at the bear and pull the trigger. Easy peasy."

"Except you forgot a little thing called loading. Not to mention aiming."

"You take all the fun out of things, you know that?"

"Well, somebody has to keep us alive. Now, shut up and keep going."

Ash mimicked Grant in a nasally high-pitched voice.

"Oh, very mature. You're just proving my point, you know."

Ash imitated him again in the same irritating voice. Grant clamped his teeth together, refusing to get drawn into a "I know you are but what am I" sort of back-and-forth with Ash he knew from experience was coming and that he couldn't possibly win. Instead, he kept forging ahead, trying to concentrate on not falling or breaking an ankle as he picked his way down the slippery side of the bluff to the plains below.

Ash seemed to think it was hilarious, though, and chuckled all the way down the bluff.

Ass.

* * *

THE RAIN WAS INTENSIFYING as they reached the outskirts of the town they'd spied while up on the bluff. Thunder boomed, and lightning lit the sky, illuminating the town. By the time they passed the first outlying building, they were both drenched to the skin.

Town, Grant thought dismally as he looked around, *might be a too-generous word for it.*

Ash seemed to be thinking the same thing—basically. "I guarantee this place has nothing but outhouses. Why does he keep sending us back to times when there's no indoor plumbing? I mean, not always, sure, but most of the time he sends us back to when the only running water is in a river and people's idea of toilet paper is a handful of leaves from the nearest bush."

Grant's mind was on other things besides bathrooms or the lack of, specifically on the lay of the town. It certainly wasn't the bustling Wild West town he'd seen in movies and television shows. It was sort of dreary and dirty and kind of sad looking.

While there were several streets, all seemed to branch off from one main one—a wide, unpaved, dirt lane that stretched east to west for several hundred yards, lined on each side by a weathered, wooden boardwalk and equally worn, wooden buildings. There was one newer-looking brick building that sported the sign "Grand Hotel and Saloon." Personally, Grant thought that name was a bit hyperbolic. He wondered how far those bricks had to be hauled because he doubted they were made locally. Whoever built the hotel probably spent a fortune having them brought in from back east. It seemed an extravagant waste of money in what otherwise looked like a poor little town.

Several hitching posts—also wooden—were spaced out along the walkway. Saddled horses were tethered to a couple of them, their heads hanging low in the rain. A pair of rough-built wagons were parked near the end of the street. Only a few people hurried along on the boardwalk—women in long dresses and bonnets, and men in faded rough-spun clothing not unlike what Grant and Ash wore. There were no children Grant could see. Maybe they were attending class in a one-room schoolhouse somewhere, or maybe this wasn't the sort of town a family would frequent. Most likely everyone with half a brain was just holed up inside one of the buildings, waiting out the storm.

The hard rain had already turned the dusty road to mud,

and as they made their way down the street, muck sucked so hard at Grant's boots he was afraid they'd get pulled right off his feet. As he concentrated on not getting stuck in the sludge, he made note of the names of the establishments in town. The place he hoped to find was a boardinghouse, somewhere he and Ash could get a room so they wouldn't have to sleep outside or holed up in someone's barn.

Not that sleeping in either of those places would be a first for them. He just thought it would be nice to have an actual bed for a change.

He patted his pocket as his gaze scanned the storefronts, and felt the reassuring lump of cash in it. Experience had taught him to keep a few dollars on him whenever Merlin sent them back in time. Merlin's magic would transform the money into currency of the day, just as it changed the clothes they wore and, at times, their hairstyles to suit and allowed them to speak and understand the language of those around them.

Not that language should be an issue here at least. Most everyone would speak English, just as he and Ash did. Well, maybe not *exactly* the same, he conceded. There might be a few colloquialisms thrown in here and there. A yeehaw, maybe. Or a yippee-kai-ay, pardner.

Urhman's Cheap Cash Store. *Probably a dry goods store. A little of everything a person might need on the prairie, from fabric to roofing nails, all in one place.* He smirked, thinking it sounded like the Wild West version of Walmart.

Across the street was a feed store, a blacksmith, and a seedy-looking establishment charmingly named the Buffalo Chip Saloon. Then he spotted a small sign in a window above the saloon and smiled. Molly's Rooming House, Beds and Meals.

Perfect. He tapped Ash on the arm. "Hey, let's head over there."

Ash's eyes flew open wide and he grinned. "To the saloon? Think they serve minors?"

He sighed and rolled his eyes. "Not to the saloon—to get a room at the boardinghouse above it. Look, there are stairs on the side of the building."

"Spoilsport. Seriously, you are no fun."

"I don't know about you, but I'm not here to have a good time. I'm here to get Butch Cassidy's gun and get home again."

"Yeah, but that doesn't mean we can't let loose a little, does it?"

"You're incorrigible."

"You know, you're right. That's exactly what it says on my court case file. Yours, too, as I recall."

Grant laughed. "You're such an ass. Come on. As soon as we get a room, we can explore this mighty city we find ourselves in."

"Why not the hotel? It's probably more comfortable than a boardinghouse, right?"

"And more expensive. Plus, they'll ask too many questions there and wonder how a couple of young cowboys like you and me can afford to stay there. The boardinghouse will be cheaper and more likely somewhere a couple of cowboys would stay."

"Great. Just what I always wanted—a trip to the Old West where we stay in the cheapest place possible."

"Not the cheapest. That would be on the ground out in the desert. Your call."

"Jeez, decisions, decisions. I guess I'll take the boardinghouse."

"That's what I thought. Let's go." He bit back a smile as Ash followed him up the stairs, grumbling all the way.

CHAPTER 2

Ash wished—and not for the first time in his life since coming to the Stanton School for Boys—it was possible for him to rip his nose clean off his face just so he wouldn't have to smell anything. In fact, he'd had cause to wish the same thing every time Merlin sent them back in time.

History, he was quickly coming to believe, stank.

Lack of sewers, lack of toilets, lack of regular baths, lack of deodorant, lack of anyone giving a rat's ass about where their horse-cow-dog-drunk neighbor took a dump—and that was only the beginning of the litany of stinkage sources Ash could list. His nose had endured it to some extent or other during every trip back so far, and this time was proving to be no different.

The odor of horseshit hit him before they even stepped foot on what passed for Main Street in the town, and only grew stronger as they progressed, eventually mixing with the stench of unwashed people, sewage, and various cooking smells. Not even the rain tamped it down—it just made everything smell wet and moldy too. He knew that soon enough he'd start to become nose-blind to the smell. That's what always happened after he'd been around it for a while—thankfully—and it would stay that way until he got a few lungsful of fresh air. Then he'd need to get used to the reek all over again.

For the moment, though, it was crisping his nose hairs.

He growled as he followed Grant up the stairs to the boardinghouse. "I swear to God, I'm going to invent air freshener. We'll be rich."

"Great. Can we find Cassidy's gun first? I'd rather go home, if you don't mind."

"Seriously? Think about it. We stay in here, in the past, and invent all kinds of cool stuff. Deodorant. Electricity. Television! We can be mega-gazillionaires."

Grant snorted at him. "First of all, I'm pretty sure electricity has been around for a while already. Second, do you have any freaking idea how television works?"

"Um, well, see there are these little, um, I mean there are..."

"That's what I thought. It's not like you can google it, you know."

"You are such a spoilsport. Really, you're a downer, man."

"I'm a realist."

"Said every pessimist, ever."

Grant chuckled and shrugged. "Maybe you're right. Anyway, game face on, okay? We have to act like we belong here"—he pointed to a small sign—"at Molly's Rooming House."

"Absolutely. Just a couple of upstanding young gentlemen who look like they took a swim with their clothes on."

"Just try not to look like you're crazy or a threat, okay?"

"I guess I can handle that."

Grant looked skeptical but, to his benefit, kept his mouth shut for a change. Instead, he rapped on the door.

A few moments later, it opened, revealing a matronly woman. She wore a long black dress, and her graying hair was braided and coiled on the top of her head. Her face, while it looked leathery, probably from having spent too many summer days under the broiling prairie sun, was open and kind. She smiled at them. "Heavens! You two look like a pair of drowned polecats. Can I help you boys?"

Grant whipped off his hat and elbowed Ash to do the same. "Um, yes, ma'am. We're in need of a room for a few nights."

Her smile tilted into a smirk. "Are you, now? And what are two fine young men such as yourselves doing knocking at my door on a night like this?"

"Well, we're just passing through, ma'am. We're real tired of traveling and can sure use a place to rest for a while. I'm afraid we're a little wet." Grant offered her what Ash knew was his most charming smile.

Ash knew it well, and it never failed to work, even on him.

It worked on Molly too. She gave them a short nod. "More than a little, from what I can see. Well, the room is a dollar a night, meals included, in advance. Now, I'll tell you that's a deal, boys. The fancy hotel down the street charges three times that, without meals."

"Yes, ma'am." Grant smiled broadly. "We'll take it."

She chewed on her bottom lip for a minute, eyeing them from head to toe as if trying to make up her mind whether she wanted them to stay. "It's Saturday. You two going to be wanting baths?"

Oh God. It was a bathe-once-a-week time in history. Ash mentally shrugged. It could be worse. They could've been sent back to a time when people thought bathing would make them sick. Talk about a stink! "Yes, ma'am. That would be great."

"It'll cost you twenty-five cents each, more if you want a shave and a haircut. You can get 'em down at the barbershop. Tell Little Eddie I sent you."

"You're Molly, ma'am?" Grant asked. He dug into his pocket and removed a few bills. Ash could see he was being careful not to let the woman know how much he actually had in his pocket.

She smirked at him as she took the money and counted it out. The bills were huge, about fifty percent larger than the dollars Grant was used to seeing. "Who else would I be? Molly McGuire, proprietress, at your service. This is seven dollars, cash money. Buys you a room and board for a week. You need to stay longer, you come see me. Now, come inside before you drown out there. It's past dinnertime, but supper is at six sharp. You want something to eat in the meantime, you can buy a steak downstairs in the saloon."

"Yes, ma'am. Could we ask what the name of this, um, fine town is?"

"Lordy! You don't even know where you are?" She shook her head and chuckled. "This is Casper, in the great state of Wyoming." She ushered them inside. "Okay, boys. This way. I'll show you to your room." She held the door open for them to pass through.

They walked into a rustic kitchen. All the cabinetry and flooring were fashioned from wood, pine from the looks of the knots in it. It was clean, if weathered and worn. The walls were bare wood as well. The only furniture was a tiny wooden table and a single chair sat on a round rag rug that was once probably colorful but now bleached gray by time. A bowl of peeled potatoes sat on the table alongside a mound of fresh peels and a knife.

Molly led them out of the kitchen and through a dining room. The walls here were covered in a flowery red fabric gone brownish in places. There was another wooden table here, fancier and larger than the other, with matching chairs, seating for eight. The rag rug underneath them wasn't nearly as old as the one in the kitchen, still retaining its bright colors. Portraits hung on the walls in ornate golden frames, photos of dour-looking people staring stiffly into the camera.

Past the dining room was a long hallway lined with doors, two to a side. She led them to the last room on the right. After opening it, she handed Ash the key. It was large and heavy, and looked like it was made from brass. He slipped it into his pocket.

"Here you go, boys. Best room in the house." Molly said it with a grin which made Ash wonder if it was really the worst room in the house. Or maybe she meant all the rooms were the same. In any case, as it turned out, her use of the word "best" was definitely open to interpretation.

The room was small, no bigger than their dorm room back at the Stanton School. There was only one bed, and it was covered over with a thick patchwork quilt. Two pillows, neither one looking anything close to being fluffy, sat propped against the wooden headboard. A bureau and a chest of drawers completed the bedroom suite.

Rain hammered against two windows, both swathed in lacy yellowed curtains. They overlooked the muddy street below. One wall held a small fireplace. Molly made short work of starting a fire in it. The heat it threw was welcome in the chilly room.

Ash knew better than to ask where the bathroom was. There wouldn't be one, not here. Instead, he grimaced when he spotted a porcelain bowl on the floor near the window. Ugh. He really hated chamber pots. He'd rather pee out the window.

It was almost as if Molly read his mind. Or maybe she'd seen him looking in disgust at the chamber pot because she hesitated at the door. "Outhouse is behind the saloon. Mind the rattlers—they like to curl up in there at night, 'specially when it's cold and rainy."

"We will. Thank you, Molly." Grant offered her that charming smile of his again.

And again, she grinned back at Grant like a freaking schoolgirl with her first crush. A momentary stab of jealousy surprised Ash, mostly because it was nuts. Molly was old enough to be their grandmother, and had the wrong plumbing to boot. Still he wanted that smile directed at him and him alone, and felt a slow burn whenever Grant aimed it at anyone else.

As soon as they were alone, Grant stripped off his clothes. Wearing only his underwear—a sight Ash appreciated even in his current drenched condition—he laid his clothing on the floor next to the fireplace to dry. He stood up, grinned, and then flung himself backward on the bed.

And practically sunk up to his chin.

"Oh, cool! It's a featherbed!" He laughed, and patted the mattress. "You gotta try this, Ash. It's more comfortable than our mattresses back home. It's like sleeping on a cloud."

Ash had his doubts but stripped off and followed suit, laying his clothing out on the floor. He laid down on the bed. "Oh yeah? I didn't know clouds were lumpy."

"It feels fine to me. In fact, I'm going to take a nap."

"No, as soon as our clothes dry out a little, you're gonna get up and go outside with me to find Butch Cassidy so we can get his gun and go home."

"Oh, right. Because it's going to be just that easy." Sarcasm was thick in Grant's voice.

Ash frowned when Grant rolled over and seemed to snuggle deeper into the mattress. He shook Grant's shoulder. "Didn't you hear what she said? There are rattlesnakes in the outhouse, Grant! Like when you were at the dude ranch! I can't take a dump when I have to worry about my ass getting snakebit. We need to go home ASAP."

"Oh, come on. We've been in worse places than this. You've gone to the bathroom outside before."

"That doesn't mean I'm yearning for a repeat performance."

He groaned when Ash shook him again. "We'll just find you a nice bush somewhere if you don't want to use the outhouse. I'll even get a big stick to protect you with."

"Is that supposed to make me feel better? You, standing guard over me with a freaking stick while I do my business?"

"No, it's supposed to make you shut up so I can take a nap. Come on. We can't go anywhere until our clothes dry out some. We'll catch pneumonia if we do."

Ash was tempted to throw himself on top of Grant and just annoy the hell out of him until he agreed to get up and explore the town, but then a strange thing happened. He realized the mattress was not as lumpy as he'd made it out to be.

In fact, it was a sort of comfortable.

Like, really comfortable. Soft and cuddly, like a hug.

Maybe, he thought just before sleep took him, *a nap isn't such a bad idea after all. Just until our clothes dry.*

CHAPTER 3

Grant woke up not remembering where he was as the last mists of sleep momentarily fogging his brain. He blinked them away and sat up in bed. Sunlight beamed in through the window. The rain must've stopped. A glance to his right showed Ash sleeping next to him, softly snoring.

So much for hurrying up and finding Cassidy. He smirked, then shook Ash's shoulder. "Hey, Rip Van Winkle. Time to get up."

Ash's drowsy, sleep-husky voice answered. "Go away. It's Saturday. No school. I can sleep in."

"It's Sunday, doofus, and we're on location, remember? Time travel? 1899? Butch Cassidy's mug shot? Any of this ring a bell?"

Ash's sleepy gaze sharpened and he sat up. "Jesus. What time is it? Is it morning? We slept the whole night!"

"Seems that way. Slept through dinner and baths. At least our clothes will be dry by now. Come on. It looks like it's still really early. Let's wash up, get dressed, and go to the kitchen to see if we're in time for breakfast. I'm starving." Grant slid out of bed and headed to the chamber pot. It wasn't optimal, but it was functional as a urinal. He sighed as he took care of his morning routine. Afterward, he washed his face and hands with water provided in a pitcher on the bureau. "Bathroom's all yours, Ash."

"Oh, funny guy. Thanks."

It didn't take them long to get ready to go, and they hurried out of the room. They passed through the dining room, which was empty and smelled strongly of bacon, eggs, and coffee.

"Shit. We missed breakfast. I need to eat, Grant. I'm starving."

"We'll find something." Grant didn't feel as positive about it as he sounded. It's not like they could just run over to the neighborhood IHOP for a plate of pancakes.

Molly was in the kitchen, scraping bits of food off a plate into the trash. A pile of dirty plates was on the counter next to her. "Well, look who's up! Breakfast was an hour ago, sleepyheads. Breakfast at 7 a.m. Dinner at noon. Supper at six."

Grant sighed and wondered if she'd think he was pathetic if he asked to lick the plates. "Yes, ma'am. We were more tired than we thought we were. We slept through supper last night too. Even missed getting our baths."

She slanted a smile at them and put the plate she held into the sink. "I had boys once, you know. They're grown and gone now, but I remember how they were at your age. Always hungry. Miss a meal or two and they'd get downright ornery. You go sit down at the table, and I'll rustle up some breakfast for you."

"Oh, Molly, that would be so great! I'm famished." Ash grinned at her and parked his butt on the only chair in the kitchen—the one next to the small round worktable.

"Not in here, fool!" She laughed at him and shooed them both from the kitchen. "Guests eat in the dining room.

Molly's rules. Go on. I'll have breakfast ready in two shakes of a lamb's tail."

Grant wondered exactly how fast a lamb could shake its tail. He hoped it was rapid-fire because his stomach was growling like a bear after a long winter's hibernation. Rather than say so, though, he kept his mouth shut and just smiled, then led Ash into the dining room. They took seats next to each other at the empty table, listening to the sounds of Molly bustling around in the kitchen.

After a while, Grant felt the urge to strike up a conversation. "What do you think we should do first after we eat? Walk around and get familiar with town?" He fiddled with the edge of the tablecloth, a well-worn but clean piece of white fabric.

"I guess..." Ash suddenly grabbed his arm. His eyes were wide, and he grinned as if he'd just had a brainstorm. "Hey! Why don't we ask Molly about Cassidy? She owns the freaking boardinghouse. Maybe he stays here when he's in town."

"That's probably the worst idea I ever heard."

Ash's excited expression collapsed like a bad soufflé. "What? Why? It makes perfect sense."

Grant sighed. "Keep your voice down! Think about it, Ash. Cassidy is a wanted man. If we ask Molly about him, she's going to think we're a pair of outlaws, too, and not to be trusted. She'd kick us out of the boardinghouse on our butts and probably report us to the sheriff to boot. We need this place. I don't want to sleep out in the desert or have to try to explain to the law why we shouldn't be thrown in jail."

"Nobody would throw us in jail just for asking a question."

"Really? This is the Old West. They hang people for stealing horses. What do you think they'd do to a pair of kids who they think have ties to America's Most Wanted?"

Ash opened his mouth but must've changed his mind about whatever he was going to say, because he closed it again and huffed out a breath.

"Look, all I'm saying is we need to be smart. We need to ask questions in a way that won't make it seem like we're trying to join the Hole in the Wall Gang."

"That's Cassidy's gang, right? Then that's exactly what we're trying to do."

Grant shrugged. "I know that, but we can't let anyone else know it."

"I guess that sort of makes sense, in a twisted, underhanded, yellow-bellied sort of way."

"Yellow-bellied? Did you actually just use that phrase in a sentence?"

"Hey, I'm fluent in Wild Western speak. *Pardner.*"

Grant snorted and had to clamp his hand over his mouth to keep from guffawing out loud. Ash had the worst western accent in the history of accents, even with the help of Merlin's magic.

They quieted when Molly came into the room bearing a large tray. She set it down, then served them plates piled high with boiled eggs, sausages, fried potatoes, and cornbread. After setting their plates in front of them, she left but returned quickly with a silver pot and a couple of cups. Soon they both had steaming cups of coffee, black and strong enough to qualify as a solid, to wash down their breakfast.

They both smiled at her. "Thanks, Molly."

"You go on and eat. Both of you are nothing more than fronts and backs with no sides. A good stiff wind would blow you clean to Laramie." She nodded and left them to their breakfast.

Ash stuffed a piece of sausage into his mouth and spoke around it. "She's a nice lady."

"Yeah, she is." Grant contemplated where to start on his

plate, then decided on a forkful of fried potatoes. It was delicious, although he was so hungry it probably could've tasted like old feet and he'd think it was manna from heaven.

They ate the rest of their meal in silence, concentrating on filling their bellies. The food was simple but good, and when he finally pushed back from the table, Grant was stuffed and ready to take on the world. Or at least, this Wild West version of it.

"So, Ash, I guess we should start by taking a walk around town. Visit the shops, keep our ears open. If Cassidy is in town or nearby, somebody is sure to mention it."

Ash shoveled the last bit of fried potatoes from his plate into his mouth. "Why would they?"

"Are you kidding? He's famous. A celebrity. It's like if we were home and heard Beyoncé or Jason Momoa was in town. It'd be all anyone would want to talk about."

"Huh. I guess you're right. Okay." He placed his fork on his plate and then belched into his fist. "I'm done. You ready to go?"

"Yup."

They both donned their hats and tried hard not to laugh at each other. Grant thought they looked ridiculous, like a pair of kids dressed up as cowboys for Halloween, and he figured from the chagrined look on Ash's face, he felt the same. Still, they would blend in, which was the most important thing, not their personal fashion sense or lack thereof.

After thanking Molly again for the impromptu breakfast, they left the way they'd entered—through the kitchen door— and trotted down the staircase to the street. The town looked different in the early morning—there were more people strolling around, for one thing. Mostly men, they noticed— cowboys dressed like themselves and a couple in fancier suits and string ties. There were a few shopkeepers who wore stained white aprons over their clothes, standing in front of their stores or sweeping the wooden walkway. . Women in long dresses and bonnets walked along in pairs, baskets hanging over their arms, some with children grabbing at their skirts. Grant noticed the women gave the Buffalo Chip Saloon a wide berth, although the men were not so discriminating.

A couple of cowboys rode horses over the muddy street, the hoofbeats muffled on the dirt road. A wagon pulled by a pair of oxen rumbled to a stop at the opposite end of the street.

Above the sounds of life in Casper, as the town went about its daily business, came jangling piano music, off-key singing, and laughter from within the Buffalo Chip Saloon.

Some people either started partying early in Casper or hadn't stopped yet from the night before, Grant thought. *Probably a little of both.*

Ash gestured toward the saloon. "Maybe we should start there."

Grant shook his head. "Seriously? The first place you want to go is the saloon?"

"Why not? Sounds like they're having a good time in there. Where do you want to go? The undertaker?" He jerked his thumb to a storefront Grant hadn't noticed before. The sign over the window read, "Hersh Brothers. Carpenters and Undertakers. Cabinetry and Coffins." There was a sample of their wares, a plain pine casket, leaning up against the side of the building. It was a little creepy to think the same guy who built your kitchen cabinets might also be building somebody's coffin at the same time.

He stifled a shudder. "Uh, no. I'd rather not."

"Good. Then the saloon it is." Ash started off toward the door to the saloon.

Unlike every saloon Grant had ever seen on television or in the movies, there was no double swinging door at the entrance. Instead, there was a wooden door with a large glass insert that read "Buffalo Chip Saloon" in gold lettering. At least, that was what he thought it said—he had to read the lettering backward because the door was being propped open by a metal milking can.

He pulled on Ash's elbows. "Maybe we should start at some of the stores. Like that clothing store. See?" He directed Ash's attention across the street to the store advertising boots, shoes, mining equipment, stationery, and hardware.

"What are you afraid of?"

Grant frowned. "I'm not afraid."

Ash shrugged. "Just seems like it. It's only a bar, Grant."

"And you've made a habit of hanging out in bars?"

"I've spent some time—"

"Oh, I cry bullshit on that."

Ash scowled and looked about to disagree, but then his frown slanted into a half smile. "Okay, so maybe I haven't been in a lot of bars."

"If by that you mean none, then okay."

"Doesn't mean we can't go in this one. Come on, Grant! We're legal here. We can get a whiskey."

Grant rolled his eyes and huffed. "Do I need to tell you how many things are wrong with that plan? First, do you even know if you like whiskey? And even if you did, what they call whiskey in the Buffalo Chip is probably closer to rotgut. It'll eat through your esophagus like turpentine. Second, we need to stay focused. The last thing we need to do is get trashed. Third—"

"Okay, okay! I get it. No drinking, Mr. No Fun McDown-erson." He paused. "If it'll make you feel better and loosen up a little, let's start at the fashion emporium across the street instead. I can't wait to see what guys are wearing when they go mining nowadays."

Grant sniffed at Ash's sarcasm but took it as a win. He

turned and led Ash across the wide dirt road to the building next to the undertaker's, aptly named the "Outfitting House."

Only three people were wandering the two aisles that comprised the whole of the Outfitting House.

One looked like an old prospector who might have panned for gold on some old television sitcom. He wore baggy, patched pants with suspenders. The cuffs were tucked inside calf-high boots, and his shirt was gray and worn. On his head was a floppy-brimmed brown hat. His beard and mustache were long and as gray as his shirt. He was perusing a selection of chisels.

The second person in the store was also male, a cowboy from the look of him. He wore sturdy pants tucked into riding boots and a plaid shirt under a long, brown duster. A hat similar to the ones Grant and Ash wore sat on his head.

Both men gave Grant and Ash a cursory look when they walked inside, then promptly seemed to forget the boys' existence.

The third person in the store was a woman. She was young, maybe their own age or a little bit older. A few curls of blond hair escaped the bonnet she wore, and her long dress was protected by an equally long apron. She was filling a basket near the counter with nails. She looked over when they entered the store, and offered them a quick smile.

"Help you boys?"

"Uh, no, ma'am. We're just looking." Grant answered her smile with one of his own.

"Well, you let me know if you find what you're looking for. We got most everything a man needs, and if you don't see it, my husband can probably order it for you from Laramie." She went back to filling the basket, shaking nails loose from the brown paper bag in her hands.

Grant tried to continue the conversation, hoping to find

out if she knew anything about Butch Cassidy. "Oh, do you own this store?"

She gave him an odd look. "My father, Elliott Phillips is the proprietor. Folks call him Grizzly. He's out back, unloading an order of planking just come in from Laramie if you need to talk to him."

"Oh, of course." Women in 1899 didn't own businesses, he realized. Or at least, not usually. "Well, we'll let you know if we find anything we need."

She nodded again and went back to her work. He and Ash moved off down the aisle, pretending to look at this item or that one. A pickaxe. A can of axle grease. Oil lanterns. Candles. Matches. On the floor were heavy bags of corn, rice, and beans. All the while they listened, to see if anyone mentioned the name of Butch Cassidy.

The only thing they heard was the occasional clomp of bootheels on the pine boards underfoot, the musical tinkle of nails emptying into the basket, and a sporadic cough from the old-timer.

"Come on. We're not going to learn anything here," Ash whispered to Grant as he placed a jar full of something black on the shelf. The label called it "fancy molasses," which made Grant wonder what ordinary molasses looked like. This stuff looked like tar.

He nodded and followed Ash out of the store. The woman didn't look up at them again, nor did either of the men in the store acknowledge their leaving.

Ash leaned against a post and folded his arms over his chest. "Now can we go to the saloon?"

Grant figured it couldn't go any worse than their trip to the outfitters, but he was still in no hurry to go into the saloon. If the bar was anything like he'd seen on television, there'd be dangerous men in there. Men who drank hard, fought often, and shot anyone who got in their way. He was in no hurry to be used for target practice. "Let's finish with the stores on this side of the street. We've got the dry goods store, the bank, and the hotel. If we don't find out anything, then we can go to the saloon."

Now Ash planted his hands on his hips, his brow furrowed. "Who, exactly, put you in charge? Because I don't remember voting you into office."

"Will you stop being such an ass?"

"Sure. As soon as you stop being so pushy."

"I'm just trying to get us home."

"You're not trying too hard. The best place to find an outlaw is in a saloon."

Grant snorted. "Says who? The last rerun you watched of *Little House on the Prairie?*"

"I don't watch that show, and I know it because I read, asshat. For your information, I've been reading Zane Grey since I was a kid. My grandfather used to read westerns, and gave 'em to me."

Surprise washed away some of Grant's irritation. "Really? I didn't know that."

Ash shrugged and leaned back against the post, shoving his hands inside his pockets. "You don't know everything about me, you know."

"Wow. I guess not. Still, those books are fiction. You can't take them as fact."

"I know that. But it still seems to make more sense than looking for Cassidy in a grocery store or a bank."

Grant grinned at Ash, waiting for him to catch on. When he didn't, he shook his head. "Cassidy robbed banks, Ash. That's actually *exactly* where we'd be likely to find him."

Ash blinked, then smirked. "See? I'm a genius."

"You didn't think of it, and you know it!"

"Keep telling yourself that. Come on. The bank's this

way." He actually had the nerve to whistle a little tune as he walked away, heading toward the Stockman's National Bank.

God, the way he could shift an argument to his benefit burned Grant's butt sometimes. It was a gift Grant didn't possess and wished he did.

Speaking of butts, Grant suddenly noticed the sweet way Ash's hitched as he walked, and promptly forgot their argument. Instead, he smiled and began to whistle too.

Sometimes you just had to be grateful for the little things in life.

The bank consisted of two rooms, one in front and another reached by a door located at the rear of the first room, behind a long counter. The counter stretched the width of the building and had several teller cages built into it, but there was only one person currently sitting behind it. He was a middle-aged man who wore his short hair parted neatly down the middle and a pair of wire-framed glasses.

He looked up from his work when Grant and Ash walked inside the bank, and waited for them to approach the counter. There was a distinct scowl on his face as he gave them the once-over, then reached over to place his hand on a pistol that sat on the counter to his right and picked it up, finger slipping to the trigger. He didn't point it at them, but the threat was clear.

"Help you boys?"

CHAPTER 4

Ash froze and put a hand out to stop Grant from passing him. "Um, yes, sir. We were hoping to open an account here."

"Were you now? Need money for that." The clerk didn't look the slightest bit convinced and didn't give any indication he was ready to put the gun down.

"We have money." Ash gave Grant a meaningful look. "Right, Grant?"

"Oh, yeah. Money. Sure." Grant slipped a hand into his pocket.

"Easy. Don't do anything stupid like pull out a knife."

Ash smirked despite the gun the clerk held. "You think we brought a knife to a gunfight? We're not stupid."

"Shut up, Ash." Grant hissed as his elbow connected with Ash's side. Then he shook his head. "Nope. Nothing like that. Just getting our money out." He tentatively slid a few bills from his pocket and showed them to the clerk. "See?"

Ash grunted and shot Grant a dark look. "Jeez. Watch it, will you? I need those ribs." He rubbed his side. That was going to leave a mark.

Grant took a few steps forward and slid the bills over the counter to the clerk.

The clerk eyed them, then finally lowered his weapon. He put the gun off to the side and counted out the bills. "There's fifty dollars here."

Grant nodded. "Yeah. We'd like to open an account, like we said."

The clerk grunted, then rummaged in a drawer under the counter, pulling out a piece of paper and inkwell and a pen. "Alright. Name?"

Ash pushed up next to Grant at the window. He was a little irritated at Grant, since Grant always seemed to take the lead on things. Plus, his ribs still hurt. "Aston Walsh."

The clerk sniffed. "Aston? What the hell kind of name is that?"

"The kind my mother gave me." Ash folded his arms across his chest and frowned.

"Yeah? Never heard it before." He sounded as if he didn't think it was a real name and wanted Ash to give another. Seriously, the guy was being sort of a dickweed.

"It's the only one I've got, and I'm kind of fond of it, so if you don't mind…" Ash jerked his chin toward the paper on the counter.

The clerk scribbled on the paper, then turned it around and slid it toward Ash. "Sign here."

The paper was a simple receipt for the amount of fifty dollars to be held in an account at the bank in Ash's name. Ash took the pen from the clerk and signed his name at the bottom of the paper. "That's all?"

The clerk took the paper and the money and rolled his eyes at them. "Unless you think I'm supposed to sing you a ditty and dance a jig, it is."

Yup. A true dickweed.

"Thanks. You know, you might want to work on your

customer service skills. Just sayin'." Ash turned on his heel and stalked out, knowing Grant would follow.

Outside, Grant smacked him on the arm.

"Ow! Will you seriously stop beating on me today?"

"I will as soon as you stop baiting the locals!"

Ash sniffed at him. "I wasn't baiting him. I was simply pointing out that he was being an a-hole."

"Look, we don't know who in town is a potential ally and who isn't. If you go around pissing everyone off, we won't get anywhere."

Ash folded his arms across his chest and put on his most sardonic smirk, the one that said he wasn't going to concede his point no matter what. "That guy is nobody's ally. He's a dickwad."

Grant threw his hands up and walked away. "You're impossible!"

"I know you are, but what am I?"

That made Grant pull up short and glare at Ash from over his shoulder. "Did you really just say that? What are you? Five?"

"I'm rubber; you're glue. Bounces off me and sticks to you." With that, Ash stuck his tongue out at Grant.

Ash could see Grant struggle to maintain his composure, but it was a losing battle. He snickered, then chuckled. "God, you're such a doofus."

"That's why you love me."

"That's not why."

Suddenly, the air between them seemed to grow heavy, making it hard to breathe. Grant had frozen, standing so still it was as if he were carved from stone. It was obvious from the shocked expression on his face that Grant had said something he hadn't meant to ever utter aloud. It was a mistake, a thought intended to be kept private, secret, perhaps not even recognized as what it was by Grant, himself. But it was out now, like a beast escaped from a cage, all sharp claws and wicked teeth, impossible to ignore.

Ash tried though. He really did.

"Um, can we go to the saloon, now? Come on. We tried your way, and we got no information we can use. It can't get any worse, right?"

Grant just shook his head, his voice a hoarse whisper. "No, I don't think it can. Let's just go."

Neither of them moved. They just stood there, trying hard not to look at each other. Ash tried to act as if nothing had happened, but his thoughts were a maelstrom of confusion. Did Grant just say he loved Ash?

Love? Like, for real?

Like the hearts-and-flowers-until-death-do-you-part love?

His eyes widened, and grew round. What should he say? What should he do? Was he supposed to say something? He didn't know what to feel, what to think, and so did what he did best. He resorted to spewing verbal vomit.

"Seriously, you're not in charge of making plans anymore. Your plans suck. We wasted all that time in a store and a bank. Cassidy is probably inside the saloon right now, playing poker and drinking whiskey or planning a bank robbery or something, and here we are wasting time with Mr. Personality there in the bank. Come on, Let's go." He strode across the street, partially hoping Grant was following and half-hoping he wasn't.

Although he struggled to put it out of his mind and pretend Grant hadn't said it, he couldn't. He was still thinking about it when he flung open the door to the Buffalo Chip Saloon and realized it was nothing like any old western he'd ever seen on television.

The Buffalo Chip Saloon looked like a dive, a wooden building worn down by time and the elements, dirty windows and a sagging boardwalk out front. The inside was no better. If anything, it was worse.

There was nothing shiny, for one thing. No glittering crystal chandeliers or polished brass rails. No spotless green-felt card tables or mustachioed, smiling piano player. Ash was willing to bet there wasn't a clean glass anywhere in the bar. No men in white hats or women in vibrant silks and feathers.

The floor was sprinkled heavily with sawdust, probably to soak up frequently spilled drinks and blood. There were several crudely built tables clustered together at one end of the single room, along with a roulette table. The seats at the tables were almost all filled with hard-looking men playing cards.

A long, equally crude bar stretched along the back wall. There were no stools at the bar—only a dull brass footrail. Evidently, the patrons of the Buffalo Chip drank their whiskey standing up unless they were playing poker.

There were a few women in the saloon, and none looked like schoolmarms. They were barely dressed, for one thing, and what little they did wear was either dingy lace or cheap satin. Their faces looked as worn as their clothing, their expressions tired and bored. They hung around in a tight little group in one corner, like a small flock of sparrows with tattered feathers.

Grant stood next to him. "Well, genius, what next?"

Obviously, he was being snarky because he was trying to forget what he'd said, which was perfectly fine with Ash but irritating at the same time. "Let's start at the bar, I guess. Talk to the bartender?"

"About what?"

Ash gave an annoyed little shrug. He really hadn't thought this through but wasn't going to admit it. "I don't know. The weather? The town? How about jobs? We can ask if he's heard if anybody around here is hiring cowboys. You know, for like, a cattle drive or something."

Grant flashed him a genuinely surprised look, which pissed Ash off. *Like I'm not bright enough to think of stuff like this? So, what does that mean? He loves me but thinks I'm stupid? What's with that?* He frowned and refused to look at Grant.

Not knowing what Ash was thinking, Grant went on blithely, pushing his luck. "You know, that's actually not a bad idea. It's something a stranger in town might ask about. Okay. Let me do the talking."

Yeah, right, because you know how to choose your words so wisely. Ash refrained from rolling his eyes, but just barely, and tried to sound as if he couldn't care less. Inside, though, anger was beginning to percolate. "Okay. Sure. Give it your best shot."

He followed Grant to the bar. Putting one foot up on the brass rail, he rested his forearms on the smooth wood surface.

Grant pulled a couple of coins from his pocket and placed them on the bar. "Barkeep? A couple of whiskeys, please."

Ash cringed inwardly. *The men in this place,* he thought, *don't look the type to say please and thank you. Their manners don't extend much past not shooting you if you give them what they asked for. Grant is going to blow this.*

Happily, the bartender didn't seem to take notice of anything except the coins on the bar top. He swept them up and pocketed them in one smooth motion. Without a word, he turned away, then returned to set two filthy glasses in front of them, along with a bottle of brown liquid. There was no label on the bottle, and no way for Ash to tell what was inside. It could've been turpentine for all he knew.

Or poison.

The bartender poured them each a generous shot, then recorked the bottle and left it on the bar between them. He turned away and began polishing a glass with a grungy rag but made no effort to hide the fact he was watching them.

Ash picked up his shot glass and waited for Grant to do the same. Then they brought the glasses to their lips and tipped the liquid down their throats at the same time.

Both of them gagged and choked.

Ash was half-convinced the stuff was turpentine. It burned like fire and tasted like if really, really bad cough medicine had been mixed with gasoline. For a long moment, he fought the urge to cough. Then he placed his glass back on the bar with a shaky hand. With a voice that sounded as if he'd been gargling glass, he said, "Smooth."

Grant nodded. There were tears in his eyes, put there, no doubt, by the burning in his belly kindled by the whiskey and his own battle not to cough. His voice sounded strangled, as if someone had their hands around his throat, squeezing. "Yeah."

A look at the bartender and the smirk on his doughy face told Ash their somewhat stoic swallowing of the rotgut whiskey hadn't fooled the man at all. He knew they were novices, newbies to the world of the saloon.

Damn it.

Grant seemed to decide to forge ahead anyway. "Bartender, we're new in town. Just passing through, you know, but we can use a way to earn some money. Do you know of anybody looking to hire a couple of hands? Maybe for a cattle drive?"

The bartender snorted. "Ain't nobody driving cattle to market at this time of year."

Grant glanced at Ash. "Oh. I see. Well, how about somebody hiring to work at a ranch?"

"You boys have experience as ranch hands?" The tone of the bartender's voice told Ash he already knew the answer, and it wasn't going to be the one Grant gave him.

"Oh, sure. Since we were kids." Grant smiled his most charming smile, the one that always made women—and Ash —weak in the knees, but Ash could see it was a totally lost effort on the bartender. His charm wasn't going to get him what they wanted this time.

"Uh-huh." The bartender continued polishing the dirty glass he held. "I don't know nobody who's hiring. I don't know where you're from, but we're going into summer, boys. Just about finished calving season. Cattle were driven down south before the snows. They'll be driven back here in midsummer."

Oh, man. We must look like a couple of real rubes to this guy. Ash stared down at his empty glass. His head was feeling buzzy, like it was full of tickling bees. He bit back a snicker at the image of bees tickling the inside of his skull with tiny feather dusters.

He eyed the brown bottle as it sat on the bar. The stuff tasted awful, but it worked like a charm, if its purpose was to get a guy plastered in one shot. His head was spinning, and he had the urge to chuckle at everything. In short, he was feeling good and toasted, like the time he'd swiped a six-pack from his dad's fridge and drank it with a couple of friends.

Right before trying to boost a car.

Which is what got him his third strike and sentenced to attending Stanton's School for Boys, which in turn landed him in Merlin's class, which led to him bellying up to a bar in 1899 Casper, Wyoming.

Oh, yeah. Drinking that stuff was probably not the best idea I ever had.

Then the bartender offered them a suggestion. "If you boys need money, you could always try your hand at panning for gold up on Casper Mountain."

"There's gold in them thar hills?" Grant snickered. His

voice sounded a little thick. He was probably feeling no pain either.

"So folks hereabouts say. You can outfit yourselves over at the—"

Grant interrupted him. "Let me guess. At the Outfitting House, right?" He sniggered again, obviously finding himself amusing.

Which, in turn, made Ash chuckle. *Grant can't hold his liquor. Look at him! He's wasted.* "Okay, let's go." He tugged on Grant's arm.

Grant teetered a minute, then regained his balance. He pointed toward the door. "Okay. To the Outfitting House!"

"Dude, remind me never to let you drink again."

"Why? I'm fine."

"You're drunk. On one shot, besides."

"I am not!" Grant paused a moment, seeming to think things over. "So are you!"

Ash chortled and led Grant—a little unsteadily—out of the saloon. "Not nearly as bad as you. Come on. Let's head back to the boardinghouse. It's probably close to lunchtime, and a little food in your stomach should help."

"We need to get outfooted."

"Outfitted. And we can do it after we eat."

"I'm not drunk."

"Maybe, but you're not sober either."

"I know you are, but what am I?"

Ash laughed aloud this time. "Touché. Now, let's go. My stomach's growling."

Keeping hold of Grant's elbow, Ash steered him around the corner of the Buffalo Chip to the stairs that led up to the boardinghouse.

To his credit, Grant only tripped once. Luckily, Ash was able to steady him before he fell down the stairs and broke anything vital. *Seriously, one shot and the dude gets royally toasted.* Ash made a mental note to tease Grant about it for the rest of their lives.

He opened the door and guided Grant into the kitchen. Molly stood at the stove, tending a pot of something that smelled delicious. She smiled at them but then frowned.

"Didn't take you boys for drunkards." Her voice dripped with disapproval.

"We're not, ma'am. We made the mistake of going into the Buffalo Chip looking for work. We should've have done it." It was sort of the truth—at least, a version of it. Ash smiled, hoping to look earnest.

"Did you get work?"

"The bartender told us to try panning for gold up on Casper Mountain."

Molly shook head and turned back to her pot. "Foolishness. Men have spent their lives trying to sieve gold out of the water up there. I suppose you're going to try it anyway?"

"We haven't talked about it yet."

"Well, I suppose you will. Most young men do, at least for a while. If you're smart, you'll try to get work with the railroad instead. Good, steady work. Honest work."

The railroad? He and Grant knew nothing about trains. Then again, they knew nothing about panning for gold, either. Still the latter seemed a lot easier than the former. "We'll talk about it. Later, after he's had some food."

She chuckled. "Food ought to soak up that alcohol. How much did you have to drink? It's only noon."

"One shot of whiskey."

Molly turned and gaped at them. "One? Truly?" She threw her head back and laughed. "Oh, God save the young and foolish!" She pointed the wooden spoon she held toward the dining room. "Go on and take a seat. Introduce yourselves to the other guests. I'll have dinner on the table in a few minutes."

Ash nodded and steered Grant toward the dining room. Grant, for his part, just smiled and winked at Molly, making her laugh again.

Ash snorted and rolled his eyes. *Even when he's drunk off his ass, he's charming.*

CHAPTER 5

Three other men sat at the dining room table when Ash and Grant came in. They'd taken seats close together at the end of the table near the window, so Ash and Grant took the seats nearest the doorway. Ash noticed the table had been set for lunch with mismatched dinnerware.

Ash nodded to the men. "Afternoon."

One of the men grunted, but the other two remained silent.

Okay. Friendly bunch. "I'm Ash, and this is Grant. We're guests here too."

One of the men, a big man with a full red beard and mustache, who wore his hair parted neatly down the middle, snorted. "Figured as much since Molly didn't brain you with her frying pan when you came in."

The other men laughed and nodded. A second man, older and grizzled, agreed. "She don't cotton to strangers coming into the house."

The third man offered his opinion. "And so she shouldn't. Not with the Wild Bunch coming into town. A woman on her own has to be careful."

The first man shook his head. "Cassidy's men don't bother nobody. Not even when they robbed that bank back home in Idaho. I heard they rode in and out again, slick as you please, with nobody getting shot."

Ash's ears perked up at the mention of Butch Cassidy's name. He leaned in and looked at the man. "I haven't heard it. What happened?"

The redhead frowned. "You dim? I just told you. Cassidy got the money, and nobody got hurt."

The first man grinned, showing Ash he was missing one of his front teeth. "Aw, don't let him bother you. I'm Bill McEvoy. This big fella is Red Andrews, and that one over there is Chance Freeman. We rode in together from Idaho because we heard there was gold, silver, and lead being mined up at Eadsville on Casper Mountain, but Molly tells us it's all but abandoned now."

"Late for the party, as usual." Chance chuckled and shook his head. "Where do you boys hail from?"

Ash's mind spun. Where were they supposed to be from? He didn't think they'd decided. What state was close to Wyoming? He tried to picture the map of the US he'd had to memorize back in grade school. "Um, we're from Indiana."

Bill nodded. "You don't say. Ain't never been there. Farm boys, were you?"

That seemed a safe enough assumption. Ash nodded. "Yeah. Both of us. Came out to find our fortunes. Just passing through here, though."

"Smart boys. You can piss from one end of this town to the other. You want to see a real city, you go on down to Laramie or Cheyenne. I hear they hold a cowboy roundup every year now in Cheyenne." Bill looked to Red as if for confirmation.

"Yup. Call it 'Frontier Days' or some such. They hold it in

July, I think. Two days long, got riding and roping events, even got them a parade."

Chance whistled through his teeth. "Hoo boy, that'd be something to see. I hear they give the winners cash money prizes, too, and silver belt buckles."

Red blew a wet raspberry. "Aw, you heard they was mining for gold and silver up on Casper Mountain, too, and look how that turned out."

Chance threw Red a wounded look. "Aw, you can't blame me for that. I was half right—they *was* mining up there. Ain't my fault the mine petered out afore we got here."

"All right, boys. No arguing at the dinner table now. It's not polite-like." Molly chided the three men like they were overgrown children. She huffed as she placed a giant bowl of stew on the table along with a ladle.

Although it smelled delicious, nobody touched it. Instead, they sat patiently waiting while Molly ran back and forth to the kitchen, bringing a basket of hot bread, a crock of fresh butter, and a pitcher of cold tea to the table.

Ash's stomach was rumbling in earnest by the time Molly finished bringing the food from the kitchen. He was already reaching for a hunk of bread when Grant's elbow caught him up short. He turned to scowl at Grant but then realized nobody else was moving yet. In fact, the three men had their heads bowed.

He caught on a heartbeat later when Molly cleared her throat and then began saying grace. He quickly bowed his head and waited quietly, if impatiently, for her to finish.

"And bless our new friends, Lord, and keep them safe and well fed. Amen."

As soon as everyone murmured amen, it was as if the entire table burst into motion at the same time. Molly laughed as they grabbed bread and held up their bowls. She filled each one to brimming with thick, hot, meaty stew.

"My, my! Folks would think you never ate before!" She smiled at them as she said it, though, making sure they knew she enjoyed feeding hungry guests. "Now, you boys chew your food. Don't need to be sending over to Doc Smith for a tonic later because you've gone and gave yourselves a bellyache."

"Yes, ma'am." Grant smiled at her. The whiskey was wearing off quickly now, Ash realized. Grant was close to being sober again, but Ash couldn't decide if that was a good thing or not. On one hand, Drunk Grant was a pain in the butt. On the other hand, so was Sober Grant at times.

The food tasted great. The stew was hot and filled with chunks of beef and vegetables. Molly's sourdough bread had a nice, crunchy crust and soft, chewy center. Ash used it to sop up the stew, and when he finally pushed back from the table, he felt as full as a tick. "Molly, you can cook for me anytime. That was really good."

Grant nodded. "It was better than any restaurant food. You're a real chef, Molly."

Bill, Chance, and Red grunted their thanks, their mouths still full of food. It seemed Ash and Grant's appetites were no match for the other three. Given the opportunity, Ash thought, between them they could probably eat a whole cow.

Grant wiped his mouth with his napkin, then pushed back from the table. "Let us help you clear the dishes, Molly."

"Oh, no. You're paying guests. You don't do my work for me. Go on, now. Supper is at six, don't forget, and I've made a sweet potato pie for dessert."

"We'll be here. Thanks, Molly!" Ash grinned at her. He and Grant both waved goodbye to the men. "See you at supper."

Bill tossed them a jaunty little salute, his mouth still full of stew and bread. The other two just grunted over their bowls.

Ash followed Grant out of the dining room and down the hall to their bedroom. He withdrew the brass key from his pocket and unlocked the door.

The room had been tidied up, no doubt by Molly, in their absence. The bed was made and the chamber pot emptied, and there was fresh water in the pitcher on the dresser.

Ash sat on the bed, then flopped back and tucked his arms under his head. "So, now what do we do?"

Grant shrugged, then sat down next to Ash. "Do you think we can trust Bill, Red, and Chance? I mean, enough to ask them about Cassidy?"

"Maybe. They seem like they're okay. Rough around the edges, maybe, and smelly, definitely, but they don't seem like bad guys."

"True enough. Okay. At supper, let's see if we can work Butch Cassidy or the Hole in the Wall Gang into the conversation. See if they have any information to share."

"What about this afternoon? Maybe we should go across the street and get outfitted as miners."

Grant blinked at him. "Why would we do that?"

Ash sighed as if Grant was an idiot. "Because then at least we'll look like we're trying to make some kind of an honest living and not just waiting around town for a group of outlaws to show up."

"Oh. Yeah, I guess you're right. Wonder how much that'll cost?"

"I have no idea. How much do you have left?"

Grant dug into his pocket and pulled out the money. He quickly counted it out. "We have eighteen dollars and fifty cents left. Do you have money?"

Ash checked his pockets. "I have a grand total of a quarter and a lint ball."

"Well, great. If lint balls are considered currency here, we're rich."

"Oh, har-har. You're a riot."

Grant snickered. "Yeah, well, I guess I'm Mr. Moneybags this trip. We can go to the Outfitters and see how much it'll cost for what we need. I guess we'd have to buy those strainer-thingees, right?"

"The what?"

"You know, the pans with the strainers on the bottom they use to pan for gold in the water."

Ash nodded. "Oh, yeah. Those thingees. Gotcha. Yeah, we're going to need two of those."

"And rope, maybe. Candles and matches."

"The guy at the store will probably know what we'll need."

"Yeah, I just don't want to get taken advantage of because he thinks we don't know what we're doing."

"But we *don't* know what we're doing."

"I know that and you know that, but he doesn't need to know it."

With a snort, Ash stood up again. "Okay, let's go do it. Then we can check out the rest of the town and maybe get in a nap before supper." He paused and shot Grant an amused smile. "By the way, you are a true lightweight. No more booze for you."

Grant's nose tipped right out of joint. "What? I am not. I was perfectly fine."

"If by 'perfectly fine' you mean perfectly drunk, then sure."

"I don't know what you're talking about. I only had the one shot."

"That, evidently, is all it takes." Ash chuckled and led the way out of their bedroom, locking the door behind them. "You, my friend, were plastered."

"I was not!"

"Think what you want, but I was there. I know better."

Ash chuckled to himself all the way down the hall, through the kitchen, and down the stairs to the street as Grant continued to grumble. He decided to let it go for now. He didn't actually want to piss Grant off—just tease him unmercifully for a bit.

They headed across the street to the Outfitters House. Inside, the same girl they'd met that morning was behind the counter, along with an older man Ash assumed was her father, the owner.

"Howdy, boys. Help you?" The man wiped his hands on a white apron he wore.

Grant offered them one of his famous smiles "Yes, sir. We were hoping to start panning for gold up on the mountain, and need equipment."

"Not much gold left up there, I reckon. Mostly played out, but if you boys want to pan the river, I got what you need." The proprietor came around the end of the counter. "Folks call me Grizzly. My daughter, Rebecca, will tally up your purchases. She's real good with her figures. Cash up front, now. We don't give no credit, you understand."

"Yes, sir. We have cash." Grant patted his pocket.

Ash was going to have to talk to Grant about advertising where he kept his cash and that he had it on him. If the wrong somebody overheard them, it might not be a stretch to imagine that same somebody robbing them later.

"All righty then. Come with me." Grizzly led Ash and Grant over to the far wall where an array of mining equipment was kept. There were pickaxes, shovels, pans, and an assortment of other items. "You'll each need one of these." He handed Ash and Grant each a gray metal pan.

The pans were the size of large pie tins and had a tight mesh bottom. Ash and Grant turned the pans over in their hands, inspecting them .

Grizzly seemed to understand they knew next to nothing

about panning for gold because he began to explain the process to them. "What you want to do is scout out a nice fat stream or slow-moving river. Find a bend in the stream— that's where the gold is most likely to pile up. You scoop up some gravel from the streambed into the pan, then hold the pan in the running water. The water washes the dirt and gravel through the holes, but leaves any gold behind. See?"

Grant nodded slowly, still looking at the pan he held. "Oh, I get it. The gold is heavier than the gravel, right?"

"That's the idea, son." Grizzly smiled at them, then started handing them more equipment. He selected a pickaxe, a length of rope, and a shovel. Then he led them around the store, picking up other items. Matches, tin cups, a pair of plates to eat on, a heavy cast-iron frying pan, a fishing rod, and something he called a parfleche, which was a rawhide container he said they could keep fish or meat in. He also selected a knife for each of them.

"I don't know, Grizzly. This seems like a lot of stuff. I don't know if we can afford it all." Grant exchanged a doubtful look with Ash.

"Well, let's see what number Rebecca works up; then we'll see what you can afford, eh?" Grizzly led them back to the counter.

Ash and Grant laid their selections on the counter and watched as Rebecca wrote each item down in a ledger along with the price in a neat, tight hand.

She offered them a quick smile, then bent her head and went to work. She paused, licked the end of her pencil, then tallied the total. "It comes to nine dollars."

Ash and Grant spoke at the same time. "Nine?" Neither could imagine spending so little for so much stuff. Back home, the shovel alone would've cost more.

"I know it's a lot, but it's all high-quality merchandise, boys." Grizzly tapped the pans, making the metal ring. "I suppose you can do without the shovel and the parfleche. Do you have knives already? We can—"

"Can you do any better on the price?" Ash thought it might be more believable if they at least pretended to try to negotiate rather than just agree to pay full price.

"Well, I'm not a rich man, and business is slow. Like I said, the gold strike petered out some of late. Not many looking to outfit themselves to pan."

"Which means you have a surplus, right?" Grant cocked his head and smiled.

"Oh, you're a shrewd one!" Grizzly chuckled. "I suppose I can take a dollar off, since you're buying two of almost everything." He held up a hand. "But only if you take it all."

Grant nodded. "Okay. It's a deal. Eight dollars for the lot."

"Deal!" Grizzly put out his hand to shake. Grant took it first, then Ash. Grizzly's handshake was firm and strong, his fingers and palm rough from a lifetime of hard work.

Rebecca's smile was broader than before. She was obviously delighted her father had made a large sale. Grizzly probably hadn't lied—business must've been slow lately.

Grant pulled out his money and counted out eight dollars. He slid it over to Rebecca. She took the money and tucked it into a cashbox kept under the counter. She brought out a large, empty flour sack and began filling it with the smaller items Ash and Grant had bought.

"Any idea where we should head?" Ash thought to ask. Grizzly probably knew the mountain as well as anyone in town. Since they bought the stuff, they might find time to actually use it. And even if they didn't, it wouldn't hurt for the townsfolk to think they were.

Grizzly nodded, as if he'd been expecting the question. "The North Platte River runs at the base of the mountain. Fishing is real good, even if you don't find gold. Tasty trout come out of the North Platte. Rainbow, brown, and cutthroat. You might start there."

Ash smiled his thanks and picked up the flour sack. It was heavier than he'd thought it would be, mostly owing to the frying pan. "Yes, sir. Thank you." He hoisted the bag over his shoulder like Santa carrying his toy sack.

Grant slipped the coil of rope over his shoulder and hefted the pickax and shovel. "Have a good day!"

"Same to you, son. Be careful on the mountain. Bears will be coming out of hibernation, and we've had trouble with wolves of late."

"And outlaws," Rebecca put in. "The Hole in the Wall Gang has been known to come into town."

"Aw, they don't bother nobody. Just stay out of their way, and you'll be fine."

"Yes, sir. Thank you."

Bears and wolves and outlaws. Something else we need to worry about, Ash thought. And Merlin still thought it was best to send them back without weapons? Well, he supposed if they were attacked, they could always whack the bear or wolf or outlaw over the head with the frying pan.

CHAPTER 6

T he sun was dipping lower on the western horizon by the time Ash and Grant had finished their self-conducted tour of the town. They discovered there wasn't much to see.

Casper had several saloons besides the Buffalo Chip. There was the "fancy" saloon in the lobby of the Grand Hotel, where gentlemen in dapper suits and polished boots played poker and roulette on tables topped with green felt. The women draped on their arms wore wedding rings, jewels, and fine dresses. This was the playground of those few who'd already made their fortunes in the area's mines, be it in gold, silver, lead, or more recently, asbestos.

The Buffalo Chip represented those at the bottommost rung of the social ladder, those who were so down on their luck they were practically horizontal, those who drank too much, gambled too much, and worked far too little. The women were prostitutes too worn or old or deep in the bottle to gain employment at any of the other brothels in town, of which there were also several.

In between were a range of other establishments bearing

names like the Silver Slipper, the Golden Calf, and the Ruby Ring, who served the middle class of Casper. They catered to those men who were employed as cowboys, merchants, or with the railroad. These men had money in their pockets, albeit not nearly the level of wealth of those who stayed at the Grand Hotel. They kept their wives and children at home, be it in town or on a ranch outside of Casper, and kept company with prostitutes from the better bordellos, like Miss Margery's or the Gardenia Garden House. They gambled and drank away their hard-earned money at the midlevel saloons.

In addition to the gambling houses and brothels, the town boasted a drug store at which remedies like Lloyd's Cocaine Toothache Drops, Bayer's Heroin-Hydrochloride Cough Syrup, and Anchor brand Laudanum for Pain Relief could be purchased, as well as soda fountain drinks. The owner—who doubled as the chemist and soda jerk—would press a tap behind the fountain to dispense syrup, then fill the rest of the glass with seltzer water. There were four flavors to choose from—vanilla, chocolate, strawberry, and I Don't Care. When Ash asked about the last one, the chemist explained the tap was filled with whatever flavor syrup they had left over from the week before. It could be vanilla, chocolate, strawberry, or more likely, some combination of all three, and always a surprise to whoever ordered it. It cost two cents less than the other flavors.

"I'm gonna live dangerously and order an I Don't Care." He grinned at Grant.

Grant was more interested in the products sold on the pharmacy's shelf than getting a fountain drink. "This can't be real, right? I mean, this one says it contains heroin! That's got to be illegal."

"Maybe not now. I don't think people knew how addictive this stuff is. It's weird though." Ash shrugged. "Not that it matters much. I don't plan on using it. Do you?"

"Hell, no. The last thing I need is to go home as an addict."

"Good choice." He slid a nickel across the counter to the pharmacist, a thin man with spider-like fingers, and watched as the pharmacist squirted syrup and seltzer water into a tall glass.

He tasted it. "Huh. Chocolate strawberry. I can live with that." He offered some to Grant, then drained the glass. "Not really cold though."

"Must be hard to keep stuff cold without refrigeration. They probably need to bring the ice down from the mountains." Grant walked to the door. "Come on. I want to see what else is in town."

Their next stop was Eddie's Barbershop, the one Molly had referred them to for their weekly bath. Grant peered through the window at two barber chairs, and further back in the shop, a curtain that was pulled back to reveal two large, clawfoot tubs.

He turned to Ash. "Hey, maybe we could get those baths now. We're getting pretty ripe."

Ash lifted an arm and took a sniff of his pit. He immediately made a face. "Yeah, I see what you mean. Okay." He rubbed his hand over his jaw. "I don't need a shave yet, though you're looking a little scruffy around the edges."

"Yeah, I was thinking of letting my beard grow."

"Ugh! No food catchers, please."

"It's not your face!"

"No, but it's the one I like to kiss." Ash grinned at him, that rakish, slanted smile that never failed to get Grant's motor running. "So, for now, how about we just get naked in the tubs?"

Grant's mouth went dry thinking about Ash's naked body, wet and slippery in the bath. He shook his head, as if to free the mental image , and nodded. His tongue suddenly felt thick. "Sure. Um. Sure. Let's go."

A bell chimed when they opened the door and stepped inside. An older man, balding and wearing a pair of round spectacles perched on his nose, came out from behind the curtain near the tubs. "Howdy, boys. I'm Eddie. What can I do you for? Looking for a shave or a haircut?" He spoke with a lilting Irish brogue.

Ash offered him a smile. "Actually, sir, we were hoping for a bath."

Eddie cocked his head. "Saturday is bath day in Casper, son. You're a day late." He gestured toward the tubs, which were empty and dry.

Grant bit his lower lip. They only provided baths on Saturday? Seriously? "Oh, I see. We just got into town yesterday. Um, okay, I guess we'll get going then. We're staying across the street at Molly's."

"Oh, Molly sent you, did she? Lovely lass, that one." Eddie considered them for a long minute. "Tell you what. Ten cents is money earned, whether it's Saturday or Sunday. You each want one?"

"Yes, sir. If you can manage it." Grant nodded.

"That'll be twenty cents, in advance. Shaves and haircuts are a nickel each." Eddie looked hopefully to Grant and Ash in turn.

Ash shook his head. "Um, I don't need a hair—"

But Grant jumped in before he could finish his sentence, surmising that their baths were going to be dependent on how much money Eddie could make from them. "Sure! We can both use shaves and haircuts." He ignored Ash's irritated scowl.

"Well, then. Good! That'll be forty cents for the two of you."

Grant was suddenly struck by inspiration. "Tell you what.

64

I'll give you fifty cents for the two of us, if you throw in some gossip."

"Gossip? Son, I know everything about everybody in town." Eddie chuckled. "That's part of what being a barber is all about. I'd chew the fat with you for free. Men tell me more than they tell their priest." He glanced at the clock on the wall, its pendulum ticking loudly. "It's getting on to suppertime. Suppose you come back after supper, say eight o'clock. I'll have the tubs filled by then."

"Excellent!" Grant grinned.

"Payment in advance." Eddie reminded them as he held out his hand.

Grant dug into his pocket and pulled out a few coins. He deposited fifty cents onto Eddie's palm. "Thanks, Eddie."

"Say hello to Molly-girl for me."

"We will." They waved as they left the shop and headed back toward the stairs to the boardinghouse.

"I think somebody has a crush on Molly." Ash chuckled as they trotted across the street.

"You think?" Grant took the stairs two at a time, and the wooden risers groaned each time he planted a foot on them. Molly was going to need a new staircase soon. This one felt as if it was getting ready to collapse. "They'd be adorable together."

"Ew. Do not put the idea of straight old people sex into my head, please."

"I never said a word about sex, you perv."

"You were thinking it."

Grant threw Ash an exasperated look. "I was not!"

"You are now."

"I hate you." But then he burst out laughing, unable to keep it in, and proved himself a liar. He didn't hate Ash. What he felt was…

Nope. He wasn't going to think about that again. Instead,

he finished climbing the stairs and let himself into the board-inghouse.

As usual, Molly was in the kitchen. This time she was frying chicken, A platter to her left was already heaped with golden brown legs, thighs, breasts, and wings, and she had another six pieces sizzling in a huge cast-iron frying pan. She looked over her shoulder when Grant opened the door, and smiled. "Chicken tonight for supper, boys. Potatoes and green beans with onions. Gravy, of course, and sweet potato pie for dessert."

"Looking forward to it, Molly." Grant cross the kitchen toward the hallway. "We're going to wash up a bit before supper."

"Oh, Eddie said to say hello for him." Ash winked at Molly. "I think he likes you."

Molly laughed, but her cheeks reddened. "Oh, that old fool? Ha! Go on, now. Supper will be on the table soon."

"Yes, ma'am." They answered in unison, then left her to her preparations.

Once inside their room, Grant sat on the edge of the bed while Ash made use of the chamber pot.

"Is it still the plan to try to bring up Cassidy at dinner?"

Grant nodded, then realized Ash couldn't see the gesture since his back was turned. "Yeah, but only if it comes up in conversation. Like, if somebody mentions outlaws or bank robberies or whatever."

"Okay."

Grant looked up as Ash stood next to him. He moved over so Ash could sit. "We might get some good information from Eddie, don't forget. I get the feeling Eddie has his ear to the ground in this town."

Ash nodded. "Yeah, I hope so. We paid for it."

"It was only another dime."

"Hey, in 1899 money, a dime is like, a thousand dollars."

Grant rolled his eyes. "It is not. A dime is maybe fifty cents in our dollars."

"In your dreams. It's worth a lot more than that! Think about it. Here, we can get a room and three meals a day for a dollar. How much do you think that would cost in our time? I'm not even talking about a Hilton or a Marriott. Say you're staying at Joe Blow's Roach Motel and eating at Mickey D's three times a day. What would it cost?"

"I have no idea. I've never stayed at Joe Blow's Roach Motel."

Ash smirked at him. "No doubt. You never stayed anywhere less than four stars, right?"

"I refuse to be goaded into defending my lifestyle."

"Oh, stop being so paranoid. Anyway, I've stayed at tons of roach motels. Let's say thirty a night. And maybe twenty bucks for three fast food meals? That makes a total of fifty bucks a day, forty-nine more than Molly charges. That means, one dollar here is worth fifty back home. That means that one dime here is worth, uh…" His eyes squeezed shut, his nose wrinkling.

How adorbs. He was trying to do the math.

Ash was handsome, funny, charming, and sexy, but math was not his strong suit.

Grant put his hand out and rested it on Ash's leg. "Ash?"

Ash opened his eyes and looked at him. "Yeah?"

"Stop before you break your brain."

With that, Grant leaned in and captured Ash's lips in a fierce kiss, effectively shutting them both up for several long minutes.

Ash tasted like a promise kept, sweet and light, sharp and tangy all at the same time. Grant was hungry for Ash's taste, denied too long. When was the last time they'd kissed? A week ago? He couldn't remember. Too long, though, for sure.

His body tightened in response, heat flaring low in his

belly, stirring things besides his feelings. He shifted his weight, making himself a little more comfortable. He slid a hand behind Ash's head, pulling Ash closer, wanting no space between them.

Ash, though, had other thoughts. He pulled away, breathing hard. "We ought to get ready for supper."

Grant gaped at him. "Seriously? You're thinking about food now?"

"No. I'm thinking about touching you. Kissing you. Doing things neither one of us is ready for."

"Who says we're not ready? You and me, we're ready. More than ready. What we have together—"

"What do we have, Grant? Do we know? I sure as shit don't, and I don't think you know, either. So, yeah. Time to get ready for supper."

It felt weird for Ash to be so hesitant. He was usually the spontaneous one. The one who took chances, who jumped in feetfirst without looking. "Does it have to be so fucking serious?" Grant lowered his gaze, not wanting to see the answer in Ash's eyes.

"I don't know. I don't know how I feel or what I want. Not yet. I don't think you do either."

Grant jumped up and walked to the other side of the room. "Don't presume to know what I think or want." He sighed and slumped, feeling the fight—and his arousal— bleed out of him. "Crap. When did you become the voice of reason?"

"The minute you obviously lost your mind."

He harrumphed but nodded. "Yeah. Okay. So, supper?"

"Yeah. Then baths. You smell like a rancid camel's ass."

"Sniff many rancid camel's asses, have you?"

"No, but I figure I'd know one when I smell one."

Grant chuckled, then shook his head. "Ass."

"That's better. Being too serious makes Grant a dull boy."

"Come on. Molly is probably putting food on the table already."

They were both smiling when they left the bedroom. But Grant's faded as he walked behind Ash to the dining room, his mind whirling as he tried to figure out exactly what he did want with Ash and how he felt. Their encounter left him feeling unsettled. Did Ash not feel about him the way he felt about Ash?

He didn't know, but he was going to have to find out. He had the feeling his heart was on the line.

CHAPTER 7

Bill, Chance, and Red were seated at the table in their usual spots. They'd been joined by a grizzled prospector with few teeth and a red-veined nose who they introduced as Pete Dawlins. Pete gave them an amicable nod but remained silent.

"Ol' Pete don't say much," Bill explained. "He keeps his own counsel, as they say."

"Aw. Is he shy? He doesn't need to worry about us." Grant offered Pete a friendly smile.

Red grunted. "Nah, Pete ain't bashful. One Eye Jackson took his tongue in a barfight a few years back."

Pete opened his mouth and wagged the stump of his tongue at them.

"Oh, ugh." Ash suppressed a shudder. "Gross. Thanks for sharing, Pete."

Grant cringed. "God, that's awful."

"Aw, don't feel bad for ol' Pete, here. He won that fight." Bill grinned and slapped Pete on the back. "Jackson wasn't called 'One Eye' afore Pete got hold of him."

Pete grinned and nodded.

Ash was suddenly very conscious of the knives set at each place setting, and reminded himself not to piss Pete Dawlins off. He very much wanted to go home with both his eyes in exactly the same place they were when he arrived.

Molly saved him from trying to decide whether he should try to remove the cutlery from Pete's reach when she entered bearing a large platter piled high with fragrant pieces of fried chicken. She placed it at the center of the table. "Now, you just keep your greedy hands off that, boys, until I get the rest of supper on the table." She said it with a smile, though, softening her words.

Ash and Grant answered in unison. "Yes, ma'am."

The other men rolled their eyes and snorted.

Bill pointed to them. "Oh, such two fine gentlemen, we got here. Always sayin' please and thank you, and yes ma'am and no ma'am. Bet they even wipe their asses politely."

Red and Chance chuckled, and Pete's odd, guttural laugh joined theirs.

"Now, don't you mind them." Molly turned to the older men and scolded them. "Stop teasing my paying guests. You three owe me a night's lodging, as I recall."

"Aw, now, Molly, you know we're good for it."

"Being good for it don't put food in my larder or money in my pocket." She sniffed and lifted her chin. "So, mind your own manners if you don't want to get the boot."

Chastened, Red, Chance, Bill, and Pete nodded. "Yes, ma'am."

Molly smiled, a bit smugly. It was obvious that she, while sweet, ruled her boardinghouse with an iron fist. "All right then. Remember what I said—don't touch that platter until I finish getting supper on the table."

No one moved an inch while she was gone.

She bustled in and out of the room and soon had bowls of green beans and onions, fried potatoes, and a plate piled with thick slices of her fresh baked bread. She took her seat at the head of the table and waited for everyone to bow their heads before saying grace.

"Amen."

The men, to their credit, didn't move toward the food until she smiled and nodded, but then it was joyous chaos as they grabbed and passed bowls, helping themselves to large portions of everything.

"Sure is good, Molly." Ash helped himself to a second piece of chicken. "Colonel Sanders has nothing on you."

"Colonel who? Did he fight for the north or the south?" Red wanted to know.

Ash blinked, then realized Red was talking about the Civil War. "Uh, I don't know. He just made really good chicken."

"But not as good as Molly's," Grant added. He shot Ash a warning look, as if to tell Ash to watch the pop culture references before they had to start explaining what country Burger was king of.

It really was good, though. The chicken was fresh and juicy, and everything else tasted just as fine. Ash ate until he was afraid he might explode if he downed one more bite. He pushed away from the table and patted his stomach. "Molly, if you keep feeding us like this we're going to get fat."

"Ha! A little more meat on your bones wouldn't hurt. I still think you're both too skinny." She smiled and helped herself to another helping of beans.

"Ash and I are going across the street to Eddie's for baths since we missed our weekly bath yesterday." Grant covered a belch with his hand—not altogether successfully—and stood up. "We'll be back later."

Chance paused with a piece of bread halfway into his mouth. "You got Eddie to fill the tubs on a Sunday? He must like you."

Ash grinned at Molly. "Oh, *we're* not the ones he likes."

Molly laughed and waved her hand at them. "Oh, go on with you, now. Go ahead, go have your baths. I'll save a couple of fat slices of my sweet potato pie for you. You can eat it later."

"Thanks, Molly!" Grant said.

Ash smiled his thanks at her, then followed Grant out of the room. Grant picked up a lantern Molly kept for her guests' use. He struck a match and lit the wick, then stepped outside.

"Ugh. I feel like a stuffed pig." Grant hurried down the stairs toward the street.

Darkness had fallen, and the stairs were treacherous in the blackness. Ash kept close behind Grant and the ring of light his lantern cast. "Yeah, me too. I meant what I said— we're gonna get fat if we keep eating like this. If they eat like this three times every day, how does everyone here not weigh five hundred pounds?"

"Think about it. Living here is hard work for almost everybody. Hauling water, chopping wood, cooking, cleaning —just surviving here burns whatever calories they take in."

"Yeah, I guess so. It's not an easy life, that's for sure."

"No, but they don't have a choice. It's normal to them. It's not like they can go to the grocery store and buy a microwave dinner, or stop for fast food on the way home from work."

Ash nodded. "Yeah, you're right. Guess we've got it easy compared to them, huh?"

They headed across the street to the barbershop. A lit lantern glowed golden in the window, telling them Eddie was in there, waiting for them.

He greeted them with a smile, wearing a white apron. Behind him at the rear of the room, hot water steamed in the two clawfoot tubs. He beckoned them to follow him to the tubs. "I have them ready for you. Nice and hot too. There's soap for each of you and a towel. Now, do you want the shave and haircut first? The water should cool a bit yet. It was boiling when I dumped it in there."

"Sure. Shaves and haircuts." Grant answered for both of them.

It made sense to Ash though. Haircut and shave, and he could wash away the itchy hairs left by both afterward in the tub. He jumped into the barber's chair, ready to go first.

"That okay with you?" Eddie asked Grant. "You paid for both. You could go first if you want."

"Nah, let him have the honors." Grant waved a hand dismissively at Ash.

"Oh, you are *too* kind." Ash made sure his voice dripped with sarcasm. It wasn't lost on Grant from the frown, however fleeting, that wrinkled Grant's forehead, and that pleased Ash to no end. He loved getting under Grant's skin. It was practically a hobby, and he was getting really, really good at it.

Eddie applied a hot wet towel to Ash's face, then after a minute or two, removed it. He slathered on cream with a brush, murmuring under his breath all the while. "Boy has less fuzz on his face than a new-hatched bird. Taking money for shaving him is like stealing from Pastor Willoughby's collection plate. Don't seem right."

Ash was about to reply something sarcastic when the blade of a straight-edge razor glinted in the lantern light. It looked wickedly sharp, and quite honestly, he wasn't altogether too convinced Eddie's hand was steady enough to wield it. One slip and he'd slit Ash's throat as easily as Molly sliced her bread. Showing a modicum of self-restraint and a great deal more interest in self-preservation, Ash kept his mouth shut.

He could hear the razor scraping his cheeks. Eddie proved to be an expert, giving Ash a closer shave than he'd ever had before. Then Eddie put down the razor and picked up a pair of scissors, and Ash began to worry all over again. After all, whatever Eddie did to his hair would carry over with him when he went back home.

Ash stared in horror at the mirror. He had been right to worry. Eddie had given him the same cut given to every one of Eddie's clients. Short all around, long on top, and parted neatly down the middle. He'd slicked it back with some sort of pomade that smelled like ass. "What did you do to me? What is that stuff?"

Eddie clucked his tongue. "Bear grease. Every man uses it 'round here. Your scalp looks stylish, but from the eyebrows down, you look like a plucked chicken. I would tell you to grow a mustache, but you'd probably have more luck growing a rose bush in the middle of winter."

Grant snickered. "I think I'll pass on the haircut, Eddie. I can use the shave though."

"Grant?" Ash's voice was little more than a squeak. There was nothing he could do at this point—the damage was done, but he was furious. He felt tricked, even though he had jumped into the chair first. "You have to get yours cut too."

"No, I don't. But don't worry, Ash. It'll grow back. Eventually." Grant's smile was almost as infuriating as the haircut.

Ash's temper broke through his shock. "Argh! I will get even, Grant. You know that, right?"

Grant laughed. "Oh, I have no doubt you'll try."

"Did you know this would happen?" Ash jabbed a finger at his own head.

"No, but I suspected it wasn't going to be like walking into the Haircuts R Us back home. Besides, you don't need to keep it parted down the middle. For now, you look like every other man down at the Buffalo Chip."

Eddie blinked. He took the razor and sharpened it by sliding the edge along a leather strop. "The Buffalo Chip?

What are you boys doing messing around in a place like that? Nothing good ever comes of it." He waved Ash out of the chair and motioned for Grant to take a seat.

"Yeah, we heard it's not the greatest place. We just peeked inside." Grant was quick to explain. He sat down and rested his hands on the arms of the chair. "We didn't gamble."

"Good thing," Eddie grumbled. He lay a hot towel over Grant's face as he'd done with Ash. "Outlaws don't even cotton to that place. Not the good ones, anyway. The Hole in the Wall Gang wouldn't be caught dead in the Buffalo Chip. When they come to town, they spend their money at the Grand Hotel or over at the Silver Slipper if they need a bit more privacy. Silver Slipper has a few private rooms, or so I hear." He removed the towel, took up the razor, and began shaving Grant's cheeks.

The mention of the Hole in the Wall Gang doused the anger simmering in Ash's gut like a splash of water on a lit match. He exchanged a knowing look with Grant. "You know the Hole in the Wall Gang, Eddie?"

"Well don't I guess so! I'm the one who gives 'em all shaves and haircuts when they come to town. Baths, too, if it's a Saturday night." Eddie chuckled. "You know, once I accidentally cut Butch Cassidy while I was shaving him. Thought I was a goner for sure. But Butch told me he'd gotten bigger cuts from counting dollar bills and a little bitty nick on the cheek was nothing. Good man, Cassidy is. Fine man. For an outlaw, I mean."

"We've, uh, heard lots about them too. Read about them in the papers." Grant glanced over at Ash as if for confirmation.

Ash was quick to agree. "Yeah, we did. They're famous."

Eddie chided Grant. "Hold still or you're likely to lose an ear. So, they made the paper all the way back in Indiana?"

76

Ash cocked his head. "How did you know where we're from? We didn't mention it."

"No." Eddie hemmed and hawed a moment, then smiled a bit sheepishly. "A certain lady fair may have mentioned it to me over a cup of ale last evening."

Grant snorted. "A certain lady fair by the name of Molly?"

"That'd be the one." Eddie grinned for a moment, then sobered. "Now, don't you boys get angry with her. She's a fine woman and trusts me to know enough to keep my mouth shut when it's important."

Ash cocked an eyebrow, sure that Eddie would keep his lips sealed only until enough coins were tossed his way. Not that he blamed Eddie, exactly. After all, he and Grant were strangers, and Eddie didn't owe them a damn thing. Still, after the haircut, he didn't harbor much generosity toward Eddie. "Uh-huh. Sure."

"Look, boys, I mean no harm. Really. All she told me was you say you come from Indiana. That's a good ways off, and I didn't realize tales of the Wild Bunch reached that far. I was surprised, that's all."

Grant offered him a smile. "It's okay, Eddie. No harm done. It's no secret where we're from. We're not wanted men. We're just two boys who got tired of the farming life and came west to find our fortunes."

Eddie nodded. "That's just what Molly said."

"I got to tell you, I sure wouldn't mind meeting Butch Cassidy and the Sundance Kid." Ash grinned at Eddie, trying to appear like a starstruck kid wanting to meet his idols. "Any chance they might come to town, Eddie?"

"Aw, they don't tell me their plans. They show up when it suits them. 'Course, now that the snows are melting on the mountains, they might come down for supplies. Lord knows those boys like gambling and women too. 'Cept for Etta Place—she's Sundance's woman—I don't think they have any women up at their camp. Of course, I don't know for sure they stayed in Wyoming for the winter. Might've gone south, you know."

Ash knew better. Merlin would not have dropped them in Casper if Cassidy and the gun weren't nearby. And that meant the Hole in the Wall Gang was close too.

"Well, boys, those baths are getting cold. Best get in 'em unless you want to end up with icicles instead of peckers." Eddie laughed as he gestured toward the two tubs in the back.

Ash and Grant exchanged a wary look, then walked hesitantly to the rear of the room where the baths they'd ordered waited. They might have been walking the last mile to the electric chair for all their enthusiasm.

"You can pull the curtain for privacy, if you want. Most men don't bother. Ain't nobody here wants to see your beans and franks." Eddie was still chuckling over his own wit as he turned away and began sweeping up hair with a straw broom. He, at least, obviously had no interest in watching either of them undress.

Ash couldn't say he felt the same. The idea of Grant stripping off in plain view and sliding into a hot tub of steamy water made him feel a little weak in the knees. Conversely, the idea of shedding his clothing down to his skin in front of Grant made him want to throw up.

What is wrong with me? I've shared dressing rooms with guys at school for years. It's no biggie, right? I mean, it's big, but not... Ugh. I'm making penis jokes in my head now? It's official. I've lost my mind.

Ash was completely relieved when Grant turned his back and unbuttoned his shirt. It seemed Grant was determined not to look, either, which was just ducky with Ash.

He turned his back as well and quickly stripped down. The sooner he got the clothes off and into the tub, the better.

Once his clothes were shed into an untidy pile on the floor, he kept his gaze cast down and stepped into the hot water. Only when he'd sunk in up to his neck did he allow himself to relax.

And tried not to think about Grant sitting naked in his tub a mere two feet away.

This is stupid. We sleep in the same room! Why is taking a stupid bath so different? He knew what it was, even if he didn't want to admit it. It was all about what Grant had said. The *L* word. Or at least, the inferred *L* word. Love. It changed everything, beginning with making him feel like a horndog when he should be feeling perfectly relaxed.

He picked up the soap and set about scrubbing himself clean, trying hard not to think about it. It was probably the quickest bath he'd ever taken. He dunked down under the water to rinse off, then grabbed the towel. Standing up, he refused to glance over to see if Grant was watching, and quickly dried off with the small, scratchy piece of fabric. By the time he dressed and finally turned around, Grant was suited up and waiting for him.

"Thanks for the baths, Eddie, and the conversation." Grant grinned at Eddie.

Ash added his thanks as well. He tried not to look at Grant. He felt awkward and weird, and all he wanted was to get to bed and start over fresh tomorrow.

"Aw, thank you, boys. Ain't often I get to make fifty cents in one shot on a Sunday." Eddie laughed. He showed them to the door. "You tell that pretty filly across the street I'm asking after her."

"We will. Night, Eddie." Grant preceded Ash out the door.

They walked back to the boarding house in silence, both of them intent on keeping their thoughts to themselves. Finally, just as they reached the stairs, Ash couldn't take it anymore.

"That was the most uncomfortable bath I've ever had."

"What? Those tubs were bigger than the ones at the dorm. I agree about the soap and towels though. Those were pretty harsh."

"I don't mean the tubs. I mean you and me. What's going on, Grant?"

Grant frowned at him. "Now isn't the time, Ash."

Ash stopped and grabbed Grant's elbow. "If not now, then when? I don't want to go through the rest of this trip feeling like this."

"Like what?"

"Like there's a wall between you and me. It feels weird and wrong."

Grant sighed. "It's my fault, okay? I'm just ready for a more physical thing and you're not, and I pushed you. That was wrong. I get it. Look, can't we just forget today happened and start over?"

"I didn't say I wasn't ready. I just don't know what I want. Is that such a crime?"

"No, it's not. And nobody should be pressured. I totally get that."

"So, we're good, then?"

Grant smiled at him, and if his grin didn't have the usual sparkle to it, it was better than a frown. "Yeah. We're golden."

He wasn't sure they were but didn't want to argue. "Good. Then let's go have sweet potato pie—whatever that is—and get some sleep. Tomorrow we need to really try to get a handle on where we can find Butch Cassidy. I don't want to be here long enough to have to get another bath."

CHAPTER 8

Morning dawned rainy and dismal. The wind swept the rain in, pelting their faces like tiny stingers. They hurried down the street, sticking to the wooden walkway as much as possible, but by the time they reached the Silver Slipper, their boots and lower pant legs were splattered with mud.

At first glance, the Silver Slipper looked little better than the Buffalo Chip had. It was housed in a nondescript wooden building, although it had a large window in front with the name *Silver Slipper* painted across it. Inside, it was marginally cleaner. The wooden floor was swept, and there weren't any dirty glasses or overfilled spittoons lying around. The furniture seemed a cut above what was available at the Buffalo Chip too. The tables were sturdier, and the roulette table had a green felt covering. The poker tables, set at the back of the room, each had a built-in seat for the dealer, a central, raised board for the cards, and chip holders.

Only one table held any action, with four men playing. The others were empty, probably because of the early hour.

Grant whispered to Ash. "What kind of poker do you think they're playing?"

"Hi-Low, looks like. See, they play five card stud, right, but the pot gets split between the highest hand and the lowest."

"Since when do you know so much about cards?"

Ash shrugged. "My grandpa taught me. We used to play on Sundays when my folks brought us to visit my grand-parents."

Grant sniffed. "All my grandpa taught me to play was the stock market."

"Seriously?" Ash rolled his eyes. "Don't you ever get tired of being the poor little rich boy?"

"Shut up."

Ash snickered, then nodded toward the table again. "Think any of them are with the Hole in the Wall Gang? I don't see Butch Cassidy."

"Me either. I guess we need to talk to them to find out."

"And how do you plan to do that? Just walk up and start chatting?"

Grant grinned at him. "No, Mister Grandpa-Taught-Me-How-To-Play-Poker. You're going to get into the game." He dug into his pocket and pulled out a few dollars. "Think this is enough? If not, I'll have to go to the bank and withdraw some."

"I'm not playing poker with outlaws."

"Well, I can't, because I don't know how. If you play, even if you lose, we may be able to get some information." Grant pushed the money at him.

Ash took the cash, albeit reluctantly. He knew Grant was right—he knew how to play, so he wouldn't look like a total idiot. At the same time, he wasn't keen on playing with a group of men all sporting revolvers in their holsters. He glanced at the bills Grant gave him. "Five bucks? That's probably enough to buy in, I think. The worst they can do is say no." He glanced at Grant. "Just do me a favor—stay close but don't make it look like we're trying to cheat. I'm pretty sure these guys take their poker seriously, and I don't want to go home dead."

Grant nodded, then followed Ash over to the table. The dealer looked up at them when they approached. "Help you, boys?"

"Got room for a new player?" Ash showed them his money. "I got five bucks burning a hole in my pocket."

A blond man glanced up. "You know how to play? We ain't got time for beginners at this table."

One of the men, a dark-haired guy with a bushy mustache, grunted. "Aw, if he's keen to lose his money, I say let him sit in, Will."

Ash forced his lips into a grin and took a chair to the man's left. "Thanks! I'm Ash. And this is Grant. We're new in town."

Another man, clean-shaven and wearing a bowler hat, spoke up. "Are we playin' poker or having a social?"

The first man shushed him. "Aw, quit it, Ben. Just 'cause we're playing ain't no reason not to be sociable." He turned to Ash. "Pleasure to meet you and take your money. I'm Kid Curry. This fine gentleman is Ben. We call him the Tall Texan, on account of him being twenty feet tall and all."

The other men laughed, and Ben grunted. Kid Curry continued. "That there is Will Carver. We're waiting on two more men, but they ain't awake yet, so you're free to play." Curry looked up at Grant. "You gonna play too?"

"Uh, no, sir. I don't know how." Grant shook his head. "I'm just watching."

Ben glared at him. "Just watchin' or planning on cheating?"

"Ben! Hesh up now. Ain't you got eyes? These two are

young enough to still be at their mama's teat," Curry chided. "I don't think they know enough to cheat!"

Will Carver spoke up. "How about we all stop jawin' and get the cards dealt?" He flipped a chip in front of him. "Ante up."

Ash knew the names, and felt adrenaline surge in his veins, kicking up his heart rate. These men were members of the Hole in the Wall Gang! Could the two men they were waiting for be Butch Cassidy and the Sundance Kid? He licked his lips nervously, wishing he could share the information and his excitement with Grant but knowing it was better to keep his mouth shut. He passed his money to the dealer, who took it and slid a double stack of chips back to him. Ash added a chip to the pot.

The dealer gave each man five cards. Curry was first up. He called.

Ash looked at his cards, careful to prevent anyone else from seeing them. A pair of deuces. Not great, but a pair was a pair. He called.

The turns went around the table, and all the players stayed in. Ash selected three cards to discard, and accepted their replacements from the dealer. A king, a queen, and another deuce. He was sitting on three of a kind. It was hard to keep a poker face and not grin like an idiot.

Curry bet two chips, and Ash matched him. The other men folded, leaving Curry and Ash the only ones left in the game. Curry bet another two chips, and Ash called again.

Curry flipped over his cards. A pair of nines, and a pair of jacks. Curry smiled smugly until Ash showed his three of a kind, and then the smile slid from Curry's face like grease from a frying pan. "How 'bout that. You win this round." He clearly wasn't happy to see Ash win. "A fella might think you was more of a player than you let on."

"Aw, it's beginner's luck," Will said. "He ain't old enough

to be a cardsharp, Kid. Tried to warn you about letting beginners sit down."

Curry grunted but didn't question Ash further. He turned his attention to the dealer. "Give us our cards."

The man complied, sliding out another hand of five cards to the players. This time, Ash drew a pair of sevens, a pair of eights, and a five. He considered his options, chewing on his bottom lip. If he kept the two pair, chances were good he might win again. If he did, Curry might decide he was cheating or a better player than he'd let on and things could get ugly quick. He didn't want to get on the bad side of the Hole in the Wall Gang before he and Grant even had a chance to meet and talk to Butch Cassidy.

He discarded both sevens and an eight, breaking up his pairs. He'd rather throw the hand than possibly piss off a man with a revolver and a temper.

The dealer slid three new cards toward him. He lifted the corners of the cards, peeking at them. He felt his stomach drop. The dealer had given him another eight and a pair of aces. He picked them up, tucked them into his hand, faced with a decision. He could play his hand and hope Curry was holding something better than his two pair, or he could pretend he had nothing and fold.

He opted for folding. Better to throw the hand than risk pissing Curry off. "I fold." He placed his cards facedown on the table and started to slide them toward the dealer when another hand clamped down over his. The hand was large and the fingers callused.

"Hold it right there, partner. Why do you want to fold? You dim in the head or something?"

Ash looked up into the face of the very man they'd been hoping to see. Butch Cassidy stood over him, a slanted smile on his lips and curiosity glinting in his eyes. "Um, I…"

"Cat run off with your tongue?" Cassidy's laugh was full and easy.

"Aw, let him fold if'n he wants, Butch." Curry frowned at Cassidy. "You ain't playing. Man's got a right to fold."

"He ain't folding. He's holding a dead man's hand." Butch flipped over Ash's cards, showing two eights and two aces.

Curry swore and threw his cards down. He had a pair of threes. "Goddamn it! Boy, you cheating? That's two in a row you won."

"I was watching him, Kid. He ain't cheating. Luck's just on his side, is all." Butch gave Ash's thin shoulder a good-natured clap that nearly knocked Ash out of his chair. He pulled another chair up, spun it around backward, and straddled it. He glanced up at Grant, then back at Ash. "What brings you boys to this fair city?"

Grant spoke up. "We came to seek our fortunes. Thought we'd pan for gold up on the mountain, but folks tell us there's not any left to find."

Ash nodded. "That's right."

"That so? If'n you're looking to make money, why are you wasting it in here playing cards?" Butch cocked an eyebrow. "Don't sound too smart to me."

"Um, yeah, well, I was hoping I could win some. I used to play with my grandpa back home when I was a kid." That much was true.

Curry blustered. "See? I knew it! I told you he was a card-sharp!" His hand strayed to his sidearm, but a look from Butch stayed his hand.

"Bull. I used to play settlers and injuns with my little brother, but that don't make me Cochise." Butch chuckled. "Seems like I come at a good time. That hand you was holding? That's called a dead man's hand on account Wild Bill Hickok got hisself shot in the back while he was holding that hand back in '76. Leastways, that's what I heard. I was only a boy myself back then."

Ben nodded. "It's true. My daddy knew a man who was there and saw it for his ownself. Man by the name of McCall done it. Was a good shot but a piss-poor gambler and a coward. Shot Bill in the back. Said Bill was holding eights and aces."

"I didn't know that." Ash swallowed hard. "Um, thanks though. I'm Ash, and this is my friend, Grant."

Butch grinned and offered his hand to shake. "Butch Cassidy. Maybe you heard of me and my men?"

"Yes, sir! The Hole in the Wall Gang. It's a real honor, sir." Grant reached over to shake Butch's hand after Ash finished.

"Aw, I hate that name!" Curry grumbled. "Folks oughtn't use it. Ain't even really a hole or a wall. Just a campsite. It ain't right. It's embarrassing, Butch."

Ash cleared his throat. "Um, well, they also call you the Wild Bunch."

Curry sat back and cocked his head. "Do they now? Well, that's more like it. I can live with that. The Wild Bunch. I like it."

Butch laughed. "Glad we got that settled. Look, Sundance went on ahead to the camp to meet up with Etta."

Will made a rude noise. "Don't know why that woman don't simply come down to town with us. Seems foolish to me."

"I'd be happy to tell her you think she's foolish, Will." Butch grinned at him. "'Course, since she's a better shot than you, it might not go so well for you when you get back to camp."

The other men laughed, and from the look on Will's face, Ash figured insulting Etta Place wasn't a smart move, even if you were one of the Wild Bunch.

"Anyway, I'm fixin' to ride out. Got big plans and lots of

details to work out." Butch looked hard at Ash and then at Grant. "Where you stayin'?"

Ash answered for them. "At Molly's boardinghouse."

Butch nodded. "Fine lady, Miss Molly is. Know'd her for a passel of years. You must be okay if she's letting you stay in her house. She don't put up with no foolishness. Listen, you say you're looking to make some money. As it happens, we're gonna need a few more hands in the coming days. If'n you're interested in joining up with us, we'd be pleased to have you."

"Now, Butch, we don't know these two from Adam. What if they're the law?" Kid Curry scowled at them. "Something smells off about 'em."

"The only thing you're smelling is your own stink because you ain't had a decent bath in over a month," Butch retorted. "You don't like who I ask in the gang, then you can just ride out."

"Nah, don't be like that, Butch. I'm just having my say, is all." Curry shook his head. He straightened his bowler hat and stood up. "I trust you, Butch. You know that."

"Okay, then. They remind me of me in my younger days, is all. So, you in, boys?" Butch looked from Grant to Ash and back again.

"Yes, sir! We're totally in!" Grant nodded so vigorously, Ash was afraid his head would fall off. It was an over-the-top performance, since Ash would bet his last nickel Grant would rather dance on hot coals than go with Butch and the boys.

Ash's reply was much more chill. Or at least, he hoped it was. His voice might have squeaked a little. "Sounds really good."

"Okay. Get your horses and meet back here in an hour. That'll give me enough time to get breakfast. I'm starving." Butch stood up and stretched, then walked toward the bar.

Ash had to wonder if Butch's intended breakfast was going to be of the liquid variety.

Ash pushed his chips toward the dealer. "Cash me in, please." He couldn't keep the excitement out of his voice. He knew he sounded like a kid who'd just been told he was going to an amusement park, but he didn't care. He was going to be an actual member of the Wild Bunch!

Grant's faked enthusiasm disappeared, and he made his worries known the moment they were outside and clear of Butch Cassidy's hearing. "What are you so pumped about? Did you miss the part about getting our horses? I hate to be the one to break it to you, but we don't *have* any horses!"

"So? We get some. The blacksmith probably has a couple we can buy."

"How about we rent them?" Grant's voice was thick with sarcasm. "We can't just stroll into the blacksmith's like it was a Hertz Rent-a-Car, order a midsize, and plop down a credit card."

"No, of course not. He'll want cash."

"Which we don't have."

"Yes, we do. In the bank. We just need to make a withdrawal."

Grant gaped at Ash as if he'd been asked to cut off his arm instead of withdrawing a few bucks from the bank. "That's all we have! What if we need money?"

"We do need money. For horses, or we're not going to be able to go with Butch to the Hole in the Wall camp. No Butch, no gun, no going home."

Grant grumbled under his breath, but Ash could tell he'd struck a nerve with his logic. And it was true. They needed to get in tight with Cassidy if they wanted a chance to get his gun. Although even then, separating an outlaw from his weapon was going to be tricky at best, and deadly at worst.

Still, they didn't have a choice, not if they wanted to go home.

"Fine, but they'd better be really cheap horses. I don't want to blow all our money on a couple of swaybacked nags."

Ash grunted, but he secretly didn't care if he had to ride a goat, as long as he got to do it as a member of the Wild Bunch.

CHAPTER 9

The bank clerk wasn't happy to see them again. He frowned under his visor, his upper lip curling slightly. "What can I do for you now?"

Ash went up to the window and tried his best to look intimidating. "I need to withdraw some money."

"For what purpose?"

Ash opened his mouth to reply, but Grant beat him to it. "That's none of your business."

"Everything is my business if it has to do with this bank." The clerk lifted his nose in the air haughtily.

"What we choose to do with our money isn't your concern. Just give us a withdrawal slip, so we can be on our way. We've got better things to do than spend the afternoon arguing with a glorified cashier. If you don't, then we'll be most happy to summon the sheriff. Withholding funds for no reason is illegal, pure and simple."

Ash had to give it to Grant—he could do condescending with the best of them. It helped that Grant came from a family with lots of money, he supposed. The clerk was hopelessly outclassed. Ash didn't know if it was illegal to withhold their money or not, but it didn't matter. The clerk was obviously intimidated by Grant's threats.

He harrumphed but slipped a piece of paper out of a drawer. "How much will you be withdrawing?"

"Thirty dollars."

The offended look on the clerk's face made it clear what he thought of Ash and Grant withdrawing such a large amount of money. He probably thought they were going to blow it in the town's saloons and brothels.

Well, let him. Like we give two craps what he thinks. Ash folded his arms across his chest and tried to match Grant's withering look of condensation. It was no contest, though, and he knew it.

The clerk took the signed paper back and carefully counted out thirty dollars from his draw. He gave Ash the money, although he still clearly wasn't happy about it. "Go on. Lose it all. Just goes to show foolish is as foolish does."

Ash was about to retort something along the lines of "takes one to know one," but Grant tugged on his arm.

"Come on. If we're going to do this, we need to move. We don't have much time."

Oh, yeah. Butch Cassidy. Hole in the Wall. Wild Bunch. Horses. Now he remembered they were in a hurry. He nodded, cast one last dirty look at the clerk, and followed Grant out the door.

They hurried down the street to the blacksmith's shop. Inside the barnlike structure, a large beefy man was working at an anvil. His forearms were as big around as Ash's thigh, and as he hammered a red hot horseshoe with a large iron hammer, red sparks fell in a shower around his feet.

He picked the shoe up with a pair of tongs and plunged it into a bucket of water. Steam hissed and rose in a cloud. "Help you boys?"

Grant nodded. "Yes, sir. We were wondering if you had any horses for sale."

The blacksmith wiped his hands on his apron. "Could be I have a couple. You going to need saddles and such?"

"Yes, sir."

"I only take cash money. No bartering, no paying terms. I ain't the bank."

"We have cash."

"Yeah? You don't look like you're men of means. Good horseflesh will cost you. Got a pair of burros you could have for a lot less."

Grant shook his head. "No, thanks. We need horses. One each, with all the trappings."

"You don't talk like cowboys."

"We're from back east."

"Ah. That explains it. Eastern folk are a strange bunch. Well, if you've got your minds set on horses, come on back. I've got a few decent rides out in the corral."

He led them through the shop and out a door where a small pen waited. In it, several horses grazed. He pointed out a chestnut and a palomino. "Now, I ain't the sort of man to send a pair of boys out to die on the prairie, and you both got the look of greenhorns on you. Ain't gonna sell you a prime stallion, no matter how much you want to pay. These two, they're easy to handle and docile. Take 'em or leave 'em. I'll need ten dollars cash money, each, and I'll outfit them each for another five dollars."

Ash grinned. That was exactly how much they had! "We'll take them!"

Grant turned and scowled at him. One of Grant's elbows connected with Ash's rib. "Jeez! Have you never heard of dickering? You never take the first price they quote you!"

"This isn't a car dealership, remember?" Ash sniffed. "You said so yourself."

The blacksmith interjected. "Eastern boys or not, my prices are fair. You won't do better anywhere else in town, or even down in Laramie. Do we have a deal? If not, I got work to do."

Grant huffed but nodded. "I guess we have a deal."

Ash just grinned but dug into his pocket and pulled out the thirty dollars they'd just withdrawn from the bank. He handed it to the blacksmith, who counted it out.

"Give me a few minutes, and I'll have them turned out for you." The blacksmith shooed them out to the shop again.

"Perfect. Now, we're broke again." Grant huffed and frowned.

"No, we aren't. We still have twenty dollars in the bank," Ash reminded him. "We're doing the right thing, Grant. We need to stick close to Cassidy if we're going to get the gun and go home."

"I know. I'm just uncomfortable with the whole thing." Grant chewed on a cuticle as they exited the shop and walked across the street to the boardinghouse. They'd need to tell Molly they were checking out. "Don't you think it was sort of weird how Butch Cassidy, this big, bad outlaw, just let two young kids he doesn't know into his gang of outlaws? It's giving me a bad feeling. Like we're being set up."

"He said he needs a few more hands, and ours were available." Ash shrugged it off. "It's probably just how they do things out here in the Wild West."

"I don't know. I think we need to be really careful from here on out."

"Okay, Mr. Doom and Gloom. Come on. We need to tell Molly we're checking out. I don't think we should tell her where we're going or who we're going with though. I doubt she'd approve of us becoming members of the Wild Bunch.

* * *

94

MOLLY DIDN'T CARE for them leaving at all. "Now, you boys just stay put right here in town. Ain't no reason for you to take off. There's good paying jobs right here. Why, I just heard Murray Tyler is hiring hands for his ranch."

"Thanks, Molly, but we really need to go. We didn't plan on staying here for long." Grant offered her a wide, warm smile. "But you've been really good to us. Thanks for everything."

Ash added his thanks. "And I'm pretty sure I've gained ten pounds. You're a really good cook"

Molly shushed them, her hands fluttering like birds. "Go on with you both! Well, if you're set on leaving, at least let me fix you a lunch to take with you. Wait right here. Won't take me a minute to put up some vittles for you."

They went to their room and gathered their few belongings, mostly the few bits and pieces they'd bought for panning gold, and stuffed them into a pair of canvas bags. Returning to the dining room, they found Molly waiting with a large brown paper-wrapped sack.

"Got you some fried chicken, a few ears of corn I roasted just this morning. There's a couple of apples in there too. I was going to make apple pie tonight, but, well, growing boys need fruit. Go on, now. And don't get yourselves snakebit or tomahawked, or fall off'n a cliff, okay?"

"Yes, ma'am." Grant took the package of food, gave Molly a peck on the cheek. She blushed like a schoolgirl, and Ash actually felt a little jealous.

"Take care, Molly."

"You too, boys. And you be sure to stop here next time you pass through."

Neither Ash nor Grant wanted to tell Molly that, if things went well, they'd never be back. It was easier and kinder to just nod and smile and take their leave.

Back at the blacksmith's, the two horses they'd bought were waiting for them, saddled and ready to ride, tethered to a hitching post in front of the shop. The saddles were thick leather, and while worn in places, they looked sturdy.

Grant and Ash used saddlebags the blacksmith provided as part of the deal to store their possessions, then mounted up.

It'd been a while since either of them had ridden, not since Merlin had sent them back to medieval Germany during the witch burnings, but it was like riding a bike. They both remembered the basics, and the blacksmith had been telling the truth—both horses were gentle and easy to ride.

They trotted down the streets to the Silver Slipper where they found Cassidy, Will, and Curry already mounted, waiting for them outside the saloon.

"See? Told you they'd be here." Cassidy grinned at them.

Curry smirked. "Guess you were right. I still don't like them coming along."

"Well, it's a good thing you don't make the rules then, ain't it?" Cassidy turned to Ash and Grant. "Ready, boys? We should make camp by nightfall if we hurry."

Without waiting for a reply, Cassidy clucked his tongue and rode toward the edge of town. The rest followed behind him, including Ash and Grant.

Ash pulled up next to Cassidy. "So, um, Butch, you said something about big plans, huh?"

Cassidy glanced at him sideways. "I did. Ain't gonna talk about it now, though. Plenty of time for that when we get up to Hole in the Wall."

"Oh, sure, sure. I understand. I was just wondering." Ash chewed on the inside of his cheek for a bit. "I heard you got arrested in Laramie a few years ago. That true?"

"Yup. I did. It was a misunderstanding, of course," Cassidy replied.

Will rode on the other side of Cassidy and laughed. "Mis-understandin'? Oh, sure it was! The law misunderstood who owned the horse he stole!"

All three men roared with laughter. "Ain't that the truth?" Cassidy shrugged. "Spent eighteen months as a guest of the Wyoming State Prison. Could've been worse, I suppose. Down in Texas, I hear they hang horse thieves. Here, I got three meals a day and a real nice tintype out of it. Remind me to show it to you when we get to camp. I think it's a real good likeness. Bought a great gun when I got out too. A Colt .45. Still have it up at the camp."

"Oh, will do!" Ash exchanged an excited glance with Grant. The gun! Butch still had it, and it was at the Hole in the Wall camp. They could be home before morning!

They rode straight through the day, stopping only twice to water and rest the horses at convenient streams. The sun was setting when they reached a protected green valley wedged between the red-colored canyon walls.

Before long, a small ramshackle cabin nestled in the shel-tered valley came into view. It had a sharply pitched roof and a short-covered porch supported by three rough-hewn logs. Two large windows graced the front of the cabin, one on each side of the front door. Each of the other three walls had one window each. A skinny black stovepipe chimney stuck out of the roof like a crooked finger. Blue smoke trailed from it in a lazy curl before quickly dispersing in the breeze.

There was a well-tended garden planted next to the cabin. Froths of greenery grew out of the earth in neat rows, although Grant had no idea what sort of vegetable they represented. A corral fashioned of the same rough logs as the cabin was in the rear. Two horses grazed peacefully within its confines. Beyond it was a barn, barely larger than the cabin.

"Welcome to Hole in the Wall, boys," Cassidy said as they

rode deeper into the valley. "That little trickle of water is Buffalo Creek. Ain't no law been able to take anybody holed up here. Anyway, Sundance should be waiting inside with Etta. Hope she's got vittles on. I'm hungry as a bear."

CHAPTER 10

G rant and Ash unsaddled their horses and turned them out into the corral, then followed Cassidy and the rest of the gang into the cabin. The inside was as raw as the outside, bare wood planks underfoot with only a few hand-woven rag rugs scattered here and there as a gesture to comfort. There was only one bed, set up next to the left-hand wall, under the window. The quilt covering it was patch-work, faded and patched. A man lay under it, his back to the door. His snores rumbled loudly in the cabin.

A black cast-iron potbelly stove was in the far corner. Its tall cylindrical stovepipe stretched up to the roof and beyond, the source of the chimney Grant had spied earlier. A fire was lit in its belly, warming the interior of the cabin and heating a large pot of something on the burner. The smell made Grant's stomach rumble, reminding him it'd been a long time since he and Ash had opened the wrapped bundle of food Molly had given them. They had shared their lunch with Cassidy, Will, Tall Texan, and Curry. While Molly had been generous, the food hadn't stretched too far considering all the hungry mouths it was feeding.

A woman, slender and pretty, stood by the stove, stirring the pot. Her dark hair was gathered up on the top of her head, and she wore a floor-length brown dress with long ruffled sleeves. It looked heavy and hot, but Grant supposed she was used to it. Women didn't wear T-shirts and shorts in 1899. She looked questioningly at Cassidy when she spotted Grant and Ash standing at the door with the rest of the Wild Bunch.

"Hey, Sundance! Get your lazy ass up," Cassidy yelled. He took off his hat and swatted the sleeping man with it. "Come on. Got two new members for you to meet."

"Goddamn it, Butch! Can't a man sleep peaceful around here?" The man sat up, rubbing his face with his hands. He looked about Butch's age, a handsome man with dark sleep-tousled hair and a thick black mustache. His blue eyes widened in surprise when he spotted Grant and Ash. "Who the hell are they?"

"Told you. Two new members of the gang. This here is Ash, and that one is Grant." Butch walked over to Etta and gave her a peck on the cheek. Then he took a deep sniff of whatever she had cooking in the pot. "Smells good, Etta. Is this your buffalo stew?"

"It is. Since when do you bring home strays?" Etta fussed at Butch, throwing a few mistrustful, unhappy glances in Ash and Grant's direction.

"Since I got big plans, and we need a few more hands. They're young, strong, and they'll do what they're told." Butch grinned at them. "Right, boys?"

"Oh, uh, yes, sir," Grant replied. He elbowed Ash, who echoed him.

"See? Ain't nobody called me 'sir' since, well, ever." Butch stole a taste of the stew from Etta's spoon and earned a swat from Etta for it. "They're right polite, these two. Say please and thank you and excuse me when they fart."

100

Sundance stood up. He wore yellowed long johns and a pair of brown pants. The pants were held up by a pair of suspenders, which he snapped as he considered Ash and Grant. "Well, ain't that perfect. A pair of real gentlemen, huh?"

"They are. A man would think they were royalty, the way they behave all genteel-like." Butch grinned and pointed at Ash. "Gonna call that one Duke and that other one there, Earl."

Ash snickered. "Earl! Oh, that's perfect."

"Shut up, *Duke*." Grant scowled at him.

"Hey, John Wayne was called Duke, and he's a legend."

"If you're John Wayne, then I'm Bruce Wayne." Grant folded his arms across his chest. He was tired, hungry, and irritable and didn't need Ash to add to his foul mood by busting his chops.

"Who are they? John and Bruce? They brothers?" Curry sat on the edge of the bed and cleaned his nails with a small pocketknife.

"Oh, yeah! I think I heard of them. The Wayne Brothers. Didn't they rob a theater once in Kansas City? Killed a little girl." Will sat next to Curry. "I don't cotton much to baby killers."

Cassidy shook his head. "Nah, you're thinking of the James Brothers, Jesse and Frank. Teamed up with the Younger Brothers for a while, and it ain't for sure true that they're the ones what pulled that job. Jesse's dead now, anyway, and I don't know where Frank is. I doubt he's one of these boys, though. He's twenty years or so older than me if'n he's a day."

Will nodded. "I remember, now. That's fine then. I don't like to ride with men who don't mind killing women and children. It's bad luck."

"You think everything is bad luck." Tall Texan, usually

quiet, spoke up. He was straddling a coarse-built kitchen chair.

"I'm just careful, is all. Why take chances? We got enough to worry on with the law on our tails." Will sniffed. He laid back on the bed, feet on the floor and arms tucked under his head, and closed his eyes. Within a few minutes, he was snoring.

Curry grimaced. "I swear, this man could fall asleep while in a wolf den and wearing a beef necklace."

Sundance huffed. "Ain't that the truth. Besides, ain't nobody after us now. We ain't pulled a job since Castle Gate back in '97."

"Don't fool yourself, Sundance. Ain't nobody forgot about us, and that's for sure." Butch shook his head and pulled up a chair. Since there were only two in the cabin and both were taken, Ash and Grant continued to stand. "We're just lucky its only the local law what's looking for us. Ain't none of them gonna try coming here."

Etta interrupted the discussion. "You boys ready to eat? Food's done." She glanced at Ash and Grant. "There're plates and spoons in the cupboard. Should be enough plates, but if we run out of spoons, you *gentlemen* can eat with your fingers."

Grant nodded. "Yes, ma'am."

Cassidy was first in line, holding his plate for Etta to fill. "Load me up, Etta. I've got a bear of an appetite today."

Etta arched an eyebrow. "When don't you?" She was smiling, though, as she spooned thick stew onto his plate and topped it with a thick hunk of bread. She did the same for Sundance, then each of the other men in turn. Ash and Grant were last, but there was plenty of food for everyone. Etta, evidently, was used to cooking for crowds.

Ash and Grant took seats on the floor in one corner of the cabin and settled down to eat. The food was pretty good.

Not five-star cuisine but not the worst Grant had ever eaten, and being hungry made everything taste better anyway. The bread was fresh and a little chewy with bits of grain, and the stew had chunks of buffalo meat, carrots, and potatoes in it.

"So, what's this big plan you got in your head?" Sundance asked Cassidy.

Cassidy spoke around a mouthful of food. "I was gonna wait until the rest of the gang gets here. Elzy, Harry, Lonnie, and Flat Nose should be here any day."

"Don't mean we can't talk about it now." Sundance sat at the table, hunched over his plate, eating with both hands. One used a fork to spear chunks of meat, and the other used a hunk of bread to sop up gravy. "I'm curious."

"Curiosity killed the cat," Cassidy replied.

"But satisfaction brought it back."

They all turned to stare at Grant, who froze with a forkful of meat halfway to his mouth. The tail end of the old saying had just blurted out of his mouth almost without him realizing it. "Um, sorry."

Cassidy chuckled. "Well, just so happens you're right, Earl. Satisfaction did bring it back. So's I guess I should tell you what I got planned. We all do our parts and it'll bring in enough to keep us in women and fine whiskey for a good long time. We should get even more than we did when we robbed the bank in Montpelier."

Sundance's eyes opened wide, and the other men sat up a little straighter. "We took in seven thousand in the job."

"Don't I know it?" Cassidy nodded happily, then got up to help himself to another serving of stew. "I expect we should get at least three or four times that much this time."

"Holy sweet Jesus on toast!" Curry sputtered. He had stew dripping from his mustache. "Just what do you plan on robbing to get that much? The danged US Treasury?"

"Nope. Guess again. This is fun." Cassidy retook his seat and started eating.

"Aw, Come on, Butch. Stop acting like a little kid with a secret and tell us." Sundance smirked. "You're enjoying this too much."

"Well, that's true. I am having fun. Okay, here it is. We, the Wild Bunch—as my good friends, Duke and Earl, have told me folks back east have named us—are going to rob the Union Pacific Overland Flyer."

Grant felt the men's excitement suddenly ignite like a pocketful of firecrackers.

"A train robbery? We ain't done one of those in a while." Curry swiped an arm across his mouth, letting his sleeve soak up the gravy from his mustache.

Sundance gave a low whistle. "The Union Pacific don't play around with folks who rob its trains, Butch. They're not going to let us just walk away."

"Don't matter. We'll get so much money we can all retire. Move someplace warm, like Mexico or down South America way, maybe. Buy a ranch, get some cattle. Live the good life." Cassidy had a dreamy, far-away look in his eyes. "Always wanted to be a cattle baron."

"Gonna take some planning to pull it off." Sundance didn't seem as excited as Cassidy, Curry, or Will, but he didn't seem against the idea either. "Lots of details to plan out. You sure these two kids are trustworthy?"

Cassidy glanced at them again. "Sure." He looked back at Sundance. "You and me can chat about them later, yeah? Besides, I don't wanna do no more planning until the rest of the gang gets here."

Sundance nodded, but Grant gave Ash a worried glance. Why did Cassidy want to talk about them to Sundance later? He got the feeling they might've gotten in over their heads, and was worried.

Ash seemed oblivious to any worry on Grant's part. Grant realized that, as a fan of old westerns, Ash was in his glory sitting here in the Wild Bunch's hideout in Hole in the Wall, hearing about the gang's plan to rob a train. He was entranced, watching the outlaws with wide eyes as he shoveled food into his mouth.

"Hey," Grant whispered, giving Ash a gentle nudge. "I'm going to go outside. Come with me."

Ash never took his gaze away from the gang. He didn't even seem to hear Grant.

"Come. With. Me," Grant hissed through clenched teeth and gave Ash another nudge, this one not so gentle. It was enough to finally get Ash's attention.

"Oh, um, okay. Yeah, I guess I gotta go too."

They set their plates down and stood up. "Back in a minute." Grant nodded to Cassidy as he shooed Ash out the cabin door.

Curry's voice, loud and obnoxious, followed them out the door. "What? One of you needs the other to hold his dick while he pisses?"

The gang guffawed in response, but Grant didn't care. He pulled Ash across the porch and around the back toward the corral.

"The outhouse is on the other side of the cabin, I think." Ash tried to walk in that direction, but Grant pulled him back.

"Listen to me. I don't have to pee. I just wanted to talk to you where they can't hear us." Grant glanced toward the cabin to make sure no one had followed them outside. "Something fishy is going on."

Ash blinked at him. "What do you mean?"

"I think Cassidy is planning to double-cross us. I don't think he's actually letting us in the gang. I think he's going to use us as, I don't know, a red herring."

"He's going to use us as a fish? That doesn't make any freaking sense."

"I mean he's going to use us as some sort of distraction when they rob the train. Or maybe as fall guys for the robbery."

Ash clucked his tongue. "Aw, Butch wouldn't do that to us."

Grant rolled his eyes. "For God's sake, think about this, Ash! Butch is an outlaw. *Outlaw.* If he was in one of those westerns you like so much, he'd be the guy in the black hat."

"Well, yeah, but—"

"Outlaws would not be above lying to get what they want or using a pair of stupid kids to take the fall for them."

Ash looked like someone had just told him there was no Santa.

"Ash, I'm sorry. I know you're excited and you want to play cowboy, but please remember we have to be careful. These men aren't our friends. We can't trust them."

"I guess. You really think Butch would throw us under the bus? Er, stagecoach?"

"In a New York minute." Grant nodded. "We just need to keep sharp and start looking for that gun and figure out how to get our hands on it. Once we have it, we're out of here."

Ash nodded, even though he didn't look in the least bit happy to have his fantasy of playing Wild West cops-and-robbers crushed under Grant's rational boot. "Okay. Come on. Let's go back inside before they start wondering what we're doing out here."

CHAPTER 11

They spent an entire week hanging around either inside or nearby the cabin while Butch and Sundance plotted the robbery, and still hadn't seen hide nor hair of Butch's Colt .45. Butch had other guns that he cleaned regularly, but none had the numbers scratched into the grip, at least not that Ash and Grant had been able to see. It had to be here somewhere. They just had to find it.

The other men took off after a day or so, riding back to Casper to get supplies, trusting Butch and Sundance to hammer out the details and fill them in when they returned. Ash and Grant stayed behind, hoping to find the revolver.

When Cassidy found out Ash and Grant could write well, he scrounged up paper and a pencil and had Grant write down their plans. They started with the facts as they knew them.

Sundance produced a map and spread it out on the small table. His finger traced the face of the map in a crooked line. "The Union Pacific train carries a lot of money on it— payroll, mostly—and keeps only one man to guard the car. For a big outfit like the Union Pacific, they ain't too bright."

It was one of the few times Ash heard Sundance chuckle. The man was usually stone-faced, the opposite of Butch's outgoing personality.

"It takes this route on its way to San Francisco," Sundance continued. "It'll pass through Wilcox in the early morning hours on June second."

Butch nodded. "Yup. They pride themselves on runnin' on time too. You can set your watch by their trains, so folks say."

"There's a little wooden bridge right about here." Sundance pointed to a spot on the map. "Just a mile or so west of Wilcox. Mile post 609, I think, or thereabouts. I reckon this is the best place for us to hit 'em. Wave 'em down with lanterns, make 'em think the bridge is washed out. They'll stop the engine for sure. Not going to risk the money going down with the train into the river."

"Makes sense." Butch frowned as if thinking hard. "Now, Union Pacific always runs the Overland in two sections, the Number One and Number Two, each of 'em pulled by an engine. Number One always carries the money, so that's the one we want. When we get Number One stopped, what happens to Number Two when it comes up behind?"

Sundance grinned. "Easy. As soon as the Number One stops, we board it and force the engineer to drive it across the bridge. Soon as it's over the bridge, we blow the damn thing sky high. The second engine won't be able to follow. It'll buy us time to get in, grab the money, and get out afore anybody knows what hit 'em."

Butch grinned. "You know how much I like blowing stuff up. It's a great plan, Sundance!"

Sundance nodded. "I figured you'd say so. I told Curry to head up to the old mine in Eadsville. There's still plenty of dynamite stored up there. Told him to bring back plenty, along with the supplies from Casper."

Butch turned to Grant and Ash. "See, boys? This is how it's done. Planning and more planning. We're careful and always stay one step ahead of the law. That's how we don't get caught."

Ash seized on the opportunity to bring up Butch's incarceration and, hopefully, the Colt .45. "You got caught once, though, didn't you? In Laramie?"

A rare frown darkened Butch's face. "That again? Look, kid, that wasn't even my fault. I was set up to take the fall for that job."

Sundance moaned as if wounded. "Aw, shit. Here we go again."

Butch ignored Sundance. "This was ten years ago, and I was barely more than a kid myself. Not much older than you two, I reckon."

Sundance snorted. "You were on your own and did your share of cattle rustling by then. Weren't you hooked up with Mike Cassidy at the time?"

"Damn straight, I was!" Butch's smile and jovial nature returned. "Mike Cassidy was a hero to me. Took me under his wing and taught me how to ride and shoot. This was just after I left home. I hired on to the Marshall ranch, and he was a hand there. By the time he was done with me, I could ride full-out in a circle 'round a tree and empty my gun into a three-inch target without missing. Took his last name as my own to honor him."

"Where did 'Butch' come from?" Grant asked. He'd been wondering ever since he found out Butch Cassidy wasn't the man's real name.

Butch chuckled. "Had me a job as a butcher's assistant for a spell. This was later, after I left the ranch, but before I went to Laramie. Folks took to calling me 'Butch,' and I guess it stuck."

"Don't let him fool you. He got the name because he fired

a shotgun named 'Butch' and got thrown back on his ass by the kick." Sundance chuckled at Butch.

"Shut up, Kid. That ain't true." Butch threw Sundance a scowl.

"Well, maybe not, but that's what some folks say."

Butch snorted. "Ain't you one to talk. You got your damn name because you spent a stretch in the Crook County Jail in Sundance, Wyoming."

"It beats getting my name because I spent my days up to my elbows in cow parts." Sundance laughed.

"So, what happened?" Grant interrupted the good-natured argument and pressed Butch. He wanted to know where the gun was so he and Grant could go home. As amusing as Butch and Sundance's banter was, it wasn't as important as finding the Colt .45. "To get you sent to prison, I mean?"

"Oh, that." Butch's smile slipped a little again. "Well, see, the cattle barons were giving the small ranchers a real hard time. Bastards had these great big herds that were taking up all the good pasture, and they were damming up streams to keep their cattle watered, leaving nothing for nobody else. I don't cotton much to those rich boys leaving nothing for the poor folks. My own ma and pa struggled hard all their lives because of men like that. Did I ever tell you we was Mormons?" Butch nodded. "It's true. Born and bred. Had us a big family, thirteen children, if you can imagine, and I was the oldest." A prideful smile lit his face. "My grandparents and parents came over from England because Brigham Young sent out a call for settlers. Took a lot of guts to uproot yourselves and travel to a land you don't know nothing about."

"Wow." Grant listened in rapt attention, unable to resist the pull of history. He could only imagine the hardships people must've faced coming across the country in the 1850s.

Ash, Etta, and Sundance seemed to be caught up in the tale too.

Butch went on. "Wasn't easy, not a bit. Had to travel in a wagon all the way from Massachusetts to Utah. It was dry, and there were awful prairie fires. Smoke so thick, you'd be hacking up a lung for miles. Granddaddy told us stories of Indian attacks and sicknesses and tornadoes ripping up the prairie. Was a godawful trip, for sure. Took 'em months. Not like now, with the Transcontinental Railroad taking you clear across the country in just a week." He got up and poured himself a cup of coffee from a large metal pot. "Anyway, after they finally got to Salt Lake City, they settled near Circleville, started up a ranch. Built that homestead with their own hands. Poured a lot of blood and sweat into it and still only barely got by.

"But then one year, my daddy had the chance to homestead a few acres of prime pastureland. It looked to make things a lot better for the family, but another settler, a big rancher, claimed homestead rights to it too. My daddy took the issue to the Mormon elders, but those sumbitches ruled in favor of the other man. My family lost everything. So, the way I figure it, if a few of the rich men's cattle went missing, it wouldn't make for much of a hardship, right? So, maybe I helped myself to a few stragglers from a herd now and then."

"Oh! So, you were a cattle rustler, then?" Grant asked.

"Aw, I didn't rustle nothing. I just helped myself when a cow or two stumbled across my path. Ain't my fault there weren't no brand on 'em. Fair game, is what I say." Butch lifted his nose in the air as if insulted. "Anyhow, the barons suspected it was me doing it but couldn't prove it. So, what they did was have a fella show me a horse and ask if I wanted to buy 'it. Now, I'm just about the best judge of horseflesh this side of the Mississippi, if I don't say so myself, and this horse was a fine specimen. Hardy, good form, and fast as lightning. Sure, I figured it was stolen, but I wasn't the one done the stealing, All I done was buy it. Paid five dollars cash money for it too."

Ash was caught up in the story. "But if you paid for them, then how did you get into trouble?"

Butch smirked. "The cattle barons claimed I stole the horse, and nothing I said made any difference. Just like when my daddy lost his land, the law sided with the rich men. I got hauled off to Laramie, put on trial, and got sentenced to two years. Made it out in eighteen months though. Good behavior."

"The *only* time he was ever good." Sundance snorted and slapped the table.

"I'd be mad as hell at you right now, Sundance, 'cept it's true." Butch laughed along with Sundance.

"And that's when you got the mug shot and gun?" Grant asked.

Butch cocked his head at Grant. "The gun?"

Ash nodded. "Um, yeah. You told us you took the mug shot from Laramie and you bought a gun after. Remember?"

"Oh, yeah, I did tell you. I remember now." Butch nodded. "Wait, I'll get it."

Grant felt frozen to his seat as Butch hurried to the bunk and scrounged underneath it. He dragged out a small metal box and used a key from his pocket to unlock the padlock holding it closed. He returned to the table carrying a small tintype and a Colt .45 revolver.

He slid the tintype toward Grant. "Lookee here. Ain't I pretty?" He laughed but then held up the gun. "Now this here gun is a thing of beauty, ain't she? Single-action army revolver, and I ain't never missed a shot with her yet."

The gun was so close, the scent of the gun oil Butch used to clean it could be detected. It was within reach, their way home! Right there, just inches away. It was all he could do not to grab for it.

There was no doubt in his mind, though, that if he did, Butch would be faster, and Grant would have a .45-sized hole in the middle of his forehead for his trouble. Besides, Merlin's magic wouldn't work until he and Ash were alone with the item. He held himself in check, but it wasn't easy. Instead, he held out his hand, trying not to let his excitement show. "Could I see it?"

Butch hesitated. "Sorry, son. I don't like other folks handling my weapons. It's like letting another man mess with your woman. Ain't polite-like." He gathered up the tintype and put the photo and the gun into the lockbox. He clicked the padlock closed and returned the box to its place under the bed.

Disappointment flooded Grant. He'd been so close! Then he reminded himself that even if Butch had handed him the gun, it wouldn't have mattered. As long as Butch, Sundance, and Etta were in the room, possession of the gun wouldn't return Ash and Grant to their own time.

At least now, they knew where the gun was. It was an important step in the right direction. He'd need to remind Ash of it as soon as they were alone. Ash looked crestfallen at the missed opportunity.

CHAPTER 12

The rest of the gang returned to the cabin a few days later, bringing not only a fresh supply of meat, potatoes, corn, flour, a few eggs, and several bottles of whiskey, but a wooden crate filled with sticks of dynamite and two new faces. Kid Curry's real-life brothers, Lonny and Johnny had arrived. The gang was complete, at least for this job, according to Butch. There were dozens of outlaws who claimed membership in the Wild Bunch, but the men present were the core.

Ash cringed at the sight of the explosives. He grabbed Grant's elbow and led him away from the wagon despite Grant's protests. He didn't stop dragging Grant away until they were behind the cabin and out of earshot of everyone else. "Listen. I'm not sure if that's safe."

"What you mean? The TNT? Nobody's going to be stupid enough to light them by accident. These guys are professionals. They know what they're doing."

"I don't mean that. How old you suppose that dynamite is?"

Grant snorted. "Seriously? You want to card the TNT?"

Ash elbowed him. "Old dynamite sweats nitroglycerin, and that makes it unstable. As in one good jolt and the whole thing explodes."

Grant's jaw went slack. "How do you even know this stuff?"

"I read."

"I doubt information like this is in comic books."

Ash sniffed in indignation. "They're *manga*, for your information, and I meant actual books. I like the Wild West. You know that. I've read some books, and I've seen documentaries. The old sticks of dynamite sweat nitro. It's true."

Grant shrugged. "I believe you. It's too weird a thing not to be true."

"Which leaves us with the question of what to do now. Do we go with them and hope the stuff doesn't blow us into the next century?"

"I don't see where we have much of a choice. They're not going to abandon their plan to blow up the bridge just because we think the TNT might not be safe."

Ash sighed. "I guess you're right, but I don't have to like it. I hope they know what they're doing."

"Yeah, you and me both. I almost wish you hadn't told me. Now I'm going to waiting for it to go boom the entire time."

"Sorry for burdening you with the truth."

"Oh, shut up." Grant smirked at him, then to Ash's surprise, ducked in for a quick kiss.

Ash's first instinct was to look around, hoping nobody had seen. The last thing they needed was for a quick kiss to out them and possibly get them bounced from the gang. They were alone though. "What was that for?"

"Being smart. And because it's been too long since the last time we kissed."

Ash smiled and leaned his forehead against Grant's. "That

was a peck, not a kiss. When we get home, remind me to teach you what a proper kiss is."

"Oh, sure." Grant laughed. "Now you're Don Juan, huh?"

"Who?"

"Says the man who claims to read history. Don Juan was a libertine who ran around seducing all sorts of women. He claimed to be a great lover."

"So, basically, a man-whore."

Grant rolled his eyes. "You're impossible."

"That's what you like most about me." Ash grinned at him. "Come on. Let's go before they start wondering what we're up to back here. Just remember to keep as much distance between your cute butt and that wagon of dynamite as you can. I want to be able to kiss all of you, not just the pieces I can find."

* * *

"You can shoot, right?"

Grant and Ash exchanged a wary look. They'd been sitting outside on the narrow porch, enjoying the few-degree drop in temperature the scant shade offered, when Kid Curry approached them. Neither knew exactly how to answer his question. If they lied and said yes, he might put them to the test where they'd be shown to be lying, but if they told the truth, they'd be admitting to be greenhorns and not worthy of membership in the Hole in the Wall Gang. It was common knowledge, they'd since learned, that Butch only asked the best of the best to be in the gang.

"Aw, take it easy on 'em, Kid. I knew they weren't gunfighters when I asked 'em to join." Butch smiled his warm, easy smile and threw an arm over Ash and Grant's shoulders. "That ain't their strong suit. These are two smart kids. Book smart. We need that. None of us had much schooling—"

Curry scowled at Cassidy. "We ain't stupid, Butch. You sayin' we're dumb?"

"*We* ain't, but *you're* dumb as mud." The other Curry was the one they called "Flat Nose." He and Kid weren't related— Flat Nose spelled his last name "Currie." Kid Curry's real name was Harvey Logan, but he adopted a variation of Flat Nose's name. So did Harvey's real brothers, Lonnie and Johnny.

Curry turned his angry glower toward Flat Nose. "Stay out of this. I'm talkin' to Butch."

"Listen, Kid, I'm not saying any of us are stupid. We ain't. We always outsmart the law, don't we? But there may come a time when we need book smarts too. Somebody who can cipher good, can read a contract, things like that. That's where these two come in." Butch clapped Ash and Grant on the back and nearly knocked them off the porch. "I figure I'll get 'em in here young, before they pick up any bad habits." He laughed, free and easy, and they all laughed with him. Butch's laugh was like that, inviting anybody within hearing distance to join in. "Anyway, I was just about to give these two fine young men a lesson in shooting, just like Mike Cassidy gave me. Come on, boys."

He led them away from the cabin, to a clearing where an old dilapidated wagon sat. It'd been there a while from the looks of things. Vines twisted through the spokes of the wagon's wheels. A few late spring wildflowers peeked between them, tiny spots of color against the dull gray wood. Spiderwebs thickened the space under the wagon not already choked by wild grasses. Jagged or missing boards made the wagon look like a mouth full of broken teeth.

While Ash and Grant watched from twenty feet away, Butch balanced a series of six empty whiskey bottles along the rim of the wagon bed. He strode back to them and drew his revolver from his holster.

Sadly, it wasn't the Colt .45 he'd shown them earlier. "This here is a Smith and Wesson Model 10 revolver. I bought it brand new just last month. Cost me twenty dollars cash money, but it's worth it. Now, it ain't my favorite, of course. That'd be my Colt .45 I showed you before, but this does the job just fine." He pointed his weapon at the wagon and squeezed off six shots in rapid succession. Each bullet shattered a bottle.

Grant felt the urge to clap. It was a cool demonstration, not only of the Smith and Wesson, but of Cassidy's ability to use it. To Grant, he didn't seem to even need to aim. It was like the gun was an extension of his body.

"Okay, who wants to go first?" Cassidy looked from Grant to Ash.

Ash, of course, being a Wild West geek, jumped at the opportunity before Grant could even form the words. "Me! I'll do it." He popped over to Cassidy's side, reaching for the gun.

Cassidy held it out to him butt-first. "First off, you need to load it." He handed Ash a handful of bullets, then showed him how to pop open the cylinder for loading. "Each bullet goes in the cylinder, like this." He demonstrated, then let Ash finish loading the other five bullets. Once the cylinder was snapped back into place, Cassidy showed Ash how to aim using the tiny sight at the end of the gun's barrel. "After you get some practice, you won't need to use the sight no more. It gets to be…what do they call it? Instinctive."

"Cool!" Ash said.

"Yeah? Sun feels hot to me. Gonna get hotter afore it gets cooler again, I reckon. You seem real sensitive to the temperature, son. You feeling okay?" Butch glanced Ash over with concern.

"Oh, um, yeah. I'm fine." Ash tilted a smile, and Grant tried not to laugh.

"Well, good then. Now, believe it or not, the fella who sold this here gun to me said a bullet fired from it will travel a thousand feet per second. Imagine that! Be like running from here clear over to the other side of the pasture in a second."

"Wow," Grant said and gave a low whistle of appreciation. The numbers were pretty impressive. Then again, that sort of speed explained how a bullet killed. Not much could stop an object traveling that fast, including the human body.

Ash didn't say anything. Grant wasn't even sure he was listening. He seemed too intent on the gun itself. "It's heavier than I thought it would be."

"Gun ought to have a heft to it, I reckon, to feel right in a man's hand. Now, don't be pointing that at nobody until I say," Butch called back as he walked to the wagon and set up six more bottles. "Don't want no accidental holes blown in my hide."

For once, Grant was happy to see, Ash listened and did as he was told, keeping the gun pointed safely at the ground until Butch returned from the wagon.

"Okay. Take aim at the first bottle. Then squeeze the trigger. Don't pull it, just squeeze." Butch put a hand on Ash's arm, helping his aim.

The gun fired, but Ash's arm jerked from the recoil and he missed his shot. He swore loudly and looked vastly disappointed.

It was much louder than Grant thought it would be, and the noise made him jump even though he'd been anticipating it. "Too bad, Ash. Good try."

"Forgot to tell you she kicks like a mule." Butch chuckled. "Got to be ready for it or your aim will be off. Go on, now, and try again."

Ash took his time, seeming to aim carefully, then squeezed the trigger again. This time, he was rewarded by the second bottle exploding into a shower of glittering glass. "Woo-hoo!" He jumped up and down like a kid who just won a prize at the state fair. "Did you see that, Grant?"

"I saw." Grant grinned at him, sharing in Ash's excitement.

"Not bad, kid. Not bad at all. Go on and shoot the rest; then we'll give your buddy a turn." Cassidy stretched out on the ground, leaned up on one elbow, chewing lazily on a long strand of straw.

Ash hit two of the remaining four bottles, and missed two. He gave a little sheepish shrug as he handed the gun to Grant. "Hit three out of five shots. Not too shabby for a first run, huh?"

"Nope." Grant smiled at him.

Cassidy jumped to his feet and hurried back to the wagon. He added three more bottles to the two Ash had left standing, then returned to where Ash and Grant waited.

Grant took the handful of bullets Cassidy held out to him.

"You remember how to load it?" Cassidy asked.

"Yeah. I was watching." Grant chewed his lower lip as he went through the steps of loading the gun. "Got it."

"Good. Remember the recoil, aim for the bottle, and let 'er loose." Cassidy returned to the ground, stretching out. He tucked both arms under his head and watched.

Grant bit his lip, taking careful aim at the first whiskey bottle. Now that he'd seen Ash fire the gun, he was expecting the kickback and was ready for it. When he squeezed off a shot, it shattered the bottle he'd aimed at.

"Whoa! Bull's-eye first time!" Ash laughed and punched Grant playfully in the shoulder. "Show off!"

Grant grinned at him, feeling proud of himself for

succeeding on his first try. He took aim at the bottles again and in short order managed to hit four of the remaining five.

"Aw, man! You got five out of six!" Ash moaned. He looked at Cassidy with a forlorn expression. "There won't be any living with him now. He'll have a swelled head."

Grant laughed. "Shut up. I'm not exactly a sharpshooter."

Cassidy chuckled along with them as he gained his feet. He took the gun from Grant and replaced it in his holster. "Give it time, boys. Give it time. I was a worse shot than either of you first time I held a gun. Just takes practice." He stretched, reaching his arms high over his head, and twisting his torso from side to side. "That's enough for today. I need to go over the plans for the train with the rest of boys. Why don't you two go make sure the horses are fed and watered?"

Grant and Ash nodded. "Sure thing, Butch. Thanks for the lesson."

"We'll do it again tomorrow." A brief frown creased Butch's forehead. "Gonna need to get you outfitted afore we go after the train. Can't have you unarmed. You got any money?"

"Not much," Grant answered. "A few dollars is all we have left."

"Well, I suppose I can front you the money. We'll go into Laramie in a few days and get you each a pistol and ammunition. Gonna need holsters, too, I reckon. Don't worry on it. We'll get you fixed up." He tossed them a good-natured salute, then strode off toward the cabin.

"You know," Ash said as they watched Butch hurry toward the cabin. "For one of the most famous outlaws in history, he's a really nice guy."

Grant nodded in agreement. "Yeah, but I get the feeling that just because he's nice doesn't mean he's not dangerous. I wonder what would happen if somebody pissed him off?"

CHAPTER 13

"I said I ain't going."

Having had to repeat himself several times, Butch's voice took on a decidedly edgy tone, one Ash and Grant hadn't heard him use before. It was sharp enough to draw blood, and the icy look in his eyes as he stared at Kid Curry left absolutely no doubt in their minds of his mood.

Curry didn't seem impressed. "What do you mean, you ain't going? It's your plan!"

"I know it. I still ain't going. I explained everything. What part don't you get?"

"None. I understand everything. I'm not stupid. What I want to know is, why you get to sit here on your ass while we take all the risks robbin' the train?" Curry was livid. His face flushed almost purple as he snarled at Butch. He was known to be the hothead of the gang, quick to temper and just as quick to shoot.

The tension between Butch and Curry grew so strained, Ash worried one of the men might pull a gun on the other. He held his breath as he stood next to Grant at the rear of the room, watching the men with widened eyes. He'd seen arguments between outlaws in movies, and they always erupted into gunfire. If it looked like one or both of them was going to draw, he was ready to throw Grant to the ground and out of the way of flying bullets.

"When I was let out of Laramie early, I got a pardon from the governor. I gave my word I wouldn't get caught doing anything against the law. If'n I do, I'll get sent to prison for so long the only way I'll leave it again is in a pine box." Butch gave Curry an unwavering stare, cold and hard. "I'm not planning to spend the rest of my life in the hoosegow."

Sundance chimed in. "Yup. It's true. I ain't crazy about the idea of him staying behind, either, Kid, but it is what it is. We got enough men to do the job. Don't need Butch."

"Don't need the leader of the gang? Whoever heard of such a thing? You think Jesse James ever stayed behind while the James Gang robbed a bank? Hell no, he didn't. He was a leader. Maybe we ought to find ourselves somebody like him to lead."

Butch jumped out of his seat so fast he tipped it over and it fell to the floor with a bang. His gun was in his hand before Curry could draw.

"You callin' me out, Kid?"

Sundance stood between the two men. "Ain't nobody calling anybody anything, Butch." He gave Curry a look that practically screamed for Curry to agree. "Ain't that so, Kid?"

Curry stared hard at the gun in Butch's hand for a long moment, then looked to the other men. "You men all right with this? With Butch staying behind?"

Each of the men either shrugged or nodded. "Ain't the first time we pulled a job on our own, Kid. Probably won't be the last," Tall Texan said. "You keep on like this, people might start thinking you're a-feared of going on your own. Are you, Kid? You need Butch to hold your damn hand? You turnin' yellow on us?"

Tall Texan's taunt was enough to push Curry over the edge. He erupted out of his seat like a rocket, pulling his gun at the same time.

He wasn't the only one, nor was he the fastest in the room. Before he could point his weapon at Tall Texan, Butch fired a shot into the ceiling of the cabin. The sound echoed in the small room, and made Ash's ears ring.

Ash shrieked and grabbed Grant's arm . He fell to the floor, dragging Grant down with him. They both hugged the hardwood planks, and Ash hoped they were low enough to avoid any stray bullet that might fly by.

"Easy, Kid. Settle down." Butch's voice remained steely, and the hand holding his gun was as steady as a rock. "Ain't nobody getting shot today. Understand?"

"He called me yella! Ain't nobody calls me a coward!" Kid yelled, looking back and forth between Butch, Sundance, and Tall Texan with venom in his eyes.

"He didn't mean it." Butch glanced at Tall Texan. "Go on. Say you're sorry and you didn't mean it."

"I ain't apologizing to nobody for nothing." Tall Texan seemed to be stuck on being stubborn. His chin tilted up, and his hand remained on his pistol's grip, although the barrel was still pointed down. Probably because Butch's was pointed at him, blue smoke still lazily drifting from the recently fired barrel.

"Yeah, you are. Nobody calls one of the gang yellow. You know that. Kid ain't no coward. He's just upset because I'm not going to be there for the robbery. I understand that—I'm the one who planned the damn thing, and it's asking a lot for men to follow that plan without being there myself and taking the same risk. But that ain't no reason to insult a man. Now, apologize." Butch's voice sounded calm, but his expression said he was dead serious.

Tall Texan grumbled but eventually mumbled an apology.

124

It was so soft it could barely be heard, but evidently it was enough for Butch and the rest of the gang.

"Okay, then! Kid, you heard him. Now, both of you, put your guns down, and let's sit and hash this out like civilized folk." Butch waited and watched with a pointed expression until both Kid and Tall Texan holstered their weapons.

As the tension in the room gradually dissipated, Ash let himself relax, finally convinced that no one, in particular him or Grant, were going to be shot. He and Grant sat up, suddenly feeling embarrassed to have hit the floor. None of the other men had ducked. They haltingly and a little awkwardly got to their feet.

To their credit, none of the outlaws in the room, rough and tough men who lived outside the law, gave Ash and Grant anything other than bored, cursory glances. Somehow, Ash got the feeling diving to the floor when a gunfight seemed imminent wasn't a cowardly act but a wise one, especially for a pair of kids who were unarmed.

He relaxed and offered Grant a small, reassuring smile. They whispered back and forth. "You okay?"

"Yeah, I'm fine. A little bruised from where you threw me to the floor, but…"

"Hmph. You're worried about a black-and-blue? I saved your life."

"Dude, please. Butch had it totally under control."

"Says you! Shots were fired!"

"Yeah, into the ceiling."

Before their hushed conversation could escalate into a shouting match, Butch spoke up again. "Now, I'm still leader of this gang, and I say there's not going to be anymore fighting amongst ourselves. That's a sure-fired way to mess things up."

Sundance tilted his chair back and put his booted feet up on the table, resting them on top of the map Butch had placed on the table earlier. "Maybe we need to go over every-thing again, Butch. Just to be sure everybody understands. I don't think Lonnie and Johnny were here when we talked about it." He tipped his chin toward Ash and Grant. "And I still ain't sure either of these two know which end of the horse shits and which one bits."

"Aw, Ash and Grant are okay. Still, I reckon it can't hurt to go over things again." Butch nodded. "Come the end of May, you're all gonna ride south and make camp outside Wilcox, milepost 609 or thereabouts, just before the bridge. You'll hide out there to wait, make sure you ain't seen. Flat Nose, you and Will are going to set the dynamite charges under the bridge, so it's ready to blow. Kid, you and Lonny are going to have the lanterns. The train is due in about two in the morning on June second. You'll use the lanterns to flag down the first train. When it stops, you'll force the engineer to drive the train over the bridge, then stop again a safe way off. Tall Texan, Will, Johnny, and Sundance will join up with you then." Butch pointed to Ash and Grant. "These two are gonna take the lanterns and go back over the bridge. They'll keep their eyes peeled for the second train."

He locked gazes with Ash, then with Grant, probably to make sure they were listening. "You two have an important job. You're gonna to flag down the second train and tell them the bridge washed out, because by the time the second train arrives, there ain't gonna be nothing left of the bridge but kindling. You don't get the second train to stop, it'll go into the wash, and the men in that train will be dead. We're robbers, not murderers. Remember that."

Kid Curry snorted. "Speak for yourself, Butch."

Butch scowled at Kid. "I am. I'm a mite proud I ain't never shot a man, and I don't intend to start now. I know the rest of you have bloodied your hands once or twice, but I haven't, and I aim to keep it that way. No killing, unless it's absolutely necessary. You got that, Kid?"

Curry grumbled but nodded. "Yeah, I hear you."

He addressed Ash and Grant again. "After you stop the train, your job is done. You jump on your horses and you ride north. You won't need to hurry as much as the others, so you don't need to worry about changing out your mounts." He pointed to a spot on the map, "Don't lollygag though. No telling what the law will do once they hear about the robbery so it's best if you don't stop again until you get back to Hole in the Wall."

"Um, how will we know the way?" Ash hated to ask— Sundance's *shits or bits* comment still stung, even if it was mostly true—but it was better to look a little stupid than be a lot lost later on.

Butch chuckled. "Sundance will point out landmarks on the way down. On the way back just keep the sunrise on your righthand side and sunset on your left. That'll keep you heading north. It'll be fifteen, twenty hours hard ride back. Maybe a bit longer because you don't know the territory. And you'll camp at least one night, rest your horses. The gang will probably beat you back here."

Turning his attention back to the rest of his men, Butch continued. "Flat Nose, after the first train stops and the boys are safely across the bridge, you blow the TNT. Then you can join the rest of the gang at the first train."

He took out a cheroot from his shirt pocket and lit it. A thin curl of blue smoke drifted up to the cabin's ceiling. "The money should be in the second car. Usually, they only have one man guarding it, but be prepared for anything. Get in, get the money, get out. We'll meet up again here at Hole in the Wall, where we'll split the loot. After that, it's every man's choice where he wants to go until the law gets tired of chasing us."

He pointed to the map spread out on the table and gestured for Sundance to move his feet. "I want fresh horses tethered here, waiting. That'll be my job, to get them there and have them waiting for you. If'n you switch out horses on the way back, you'll get back here sooner. Won't need to wait to rest and water the ones you ride down." He smirked. "Still can't believe the law ain't caught on to my little trick yet. They'll have to stop a couple of times on the way. It'll turn a fifteen-hour hard ride into a two-day trip. Makes you wonder how bright they are. Anyway, it really don't matter none. We'll be settled up and gone before they even know the train was robbed."

All the men, Ash and Grant included, nodded their understanding.

"Anybody got any questions?"

None of the gang voiced any. Kid Curry didn't look particularly happy, but then, he never did. At least his weapon remained holstered and his mouth stayed shut. Ash counted it as a win.

Grant cleared his throat. "Um, what do we do until then, Butch? We've still got two weeks until the end of May."

"You're gonna do exactly what you done today. Learn to shoot. Work on your horsemanship. You ain't the riders you need to be yet. I'm not sending either one of you boys on a job until you can pick off six bottles out of six without a miss and ride a horse like you was attached to the saddle by the ass."

Ash and Grant both nodded. Suddenly, Ash realized there might be a way to get his hands on Butch's Colt .45, and he would've grinned if he hadn't remembered to pull it back in time. The men might think he was bonkers if he seemed to get so excited about target practice, but it was hard to keep from smiling. "It might go faster if we could both practice at the same time, Butch. Maybe there's an extra gun around that we can use?"

Grant caught on quickly. "Yeah, exactly. Like, maybe the one in the box under your bed? I mean, nobody's using it, right?"

Butch shot them down—figuratively. "Not a chance, son. That's my lucky gun, and I don't lend it out. 'Sides, I need to watch each of you shoot to give you pointers." He grinned. "Truth be told, I don't trust neither one of you not to shoot the other on accident if I ain't watching."

* * *

EACH DAY WAS DIVIDED into two halves—shooting and riding. They practiced shooting first each day, first at bottles, then at targets crudely drawn on fence poles, going on for hours until their hands felt numb from firing the revolver so many times. Their shoulders throbbed from the repeated kick-backs, and the muscles in their forearms ached from holding the gun up and keeping it steady for so long, but their aim slowly improved. Before not too many days had passed, they were hitting the targets more than they were missing.

The second half of the day was spent on horseback, and Ash's butt felt permanently bruised by the end of the first week. Still, he had to admit he was far more comfortable in the saddle than he'd been earlier.

They were at target practice again. Under the brilliant rays of an unforgiving sun, bits of broken glass glittered on the ground surrounding the old wagon. It looked as if the skies had rained diamonds the night before. It was both beautiful and telling, since it was evidence of how hard Ash and Grant were working to reach the goal Butch had set for them.

"Damn it! I almost got them all that time!" Ash kicked a

rock toward the wagon. It skittered over broken glass until it rolled to stop at one of the broken wheels.

"Don't worry. You'll get there." Grant felt a little smug since he'd progressed faster than Ash. He could shoot six out of six almost every time. It wouldn't be long before he didn't miss anymore at all, but Ash still had a way to go.

Ash grumbled. "Oh, shut up, Grant. You're just lucky, that's all. Besides, it's not a competition, you know."

"Said every loser, ever." Grant laughed. He blew a breath of air over the gun's muzzle like an old-time movie cowboy. "I'm a dead shot. Hey! Maybe that should be my outlaw name. Dead Shot."

"Dead *Snot*, maybe," Ash shot back. He took the gun from Grant's hand and reloaded it.

"Oh, how clever." Grant sniffed. "Pure comic gold. Not."

Ash didn't bother with a retort. Instead, he took aim and began shooting again. This time, he shattered all six bottles. "Ha! Told you! All six!"

"Well, good for you." Grant's voice dripped sarcasm. "Of course, the law of averages says you'd get them all eventually."

"Okay, okay. Enough!" Butch laughed and walked between them. He took his gun back from Ash and holstered it. "You both have been doin' real good. Now, saddle up your horses."

"Can we eat first? We usually don't start riding until after lunch."

"Nope. We're gonna take a ride into Laramie, and its going to take us a few days to make the trip there and back. It's a sight further than Wilcox, through some rough country."

Grant and Ash exchanged a surprised look. "Laramie? Why are we going there?"

"Well, you ain't gonna keep taking turns shooting my gun

forever, are you?" Butch offered them a wide smile. "Gonna go buy you each your own. Now, go on. Don't forget your bedrolls."

Grant grinned his widest smile. "Awesome!"

"What he said!" Ash laughed and then took off running toward the cabin. He and Grant grabbed their bedrolls— their eating utensils and other possessions rolled up tightly in a blanket—and then dashed for the corral where the horses grazed. Ash could see Grant's excitement in his wide grin, and it matched his own. They'd heard about Laramie and were almost as excited to see what passed for a bustling city in the Wild West as they were to get their own weapons.

CHAPTER 14

L aramie was much more of a city than either Ash or Grant had expected it to be. The streets, although unpaved, were very wide, and most of the buildings were two-story brick. Gleaming glass display windows glinted in the sunlight. Instead of basic goods for sale, Laramie offered more specialized shops, some of which advertised luxuries like fragranced soaps, perfumes, and crystal. As they walked down Second Street, they came across W. H. Williston's Stationery and Book Store, Star Clothiers, Still Brothers Bakery, and something called the Temple of Economy, which Grant thought might be a bank.

The population here seemed much more well-to-do than they'd been in Casper, not counting the wealthy people at the Grand Hotel. Men and women strolled along the raised wooden walkway on each side of the street, dressed in much finer clothing than what most folks back in Casper had been wearing. The colors were brighter, and the fabrics seemed newer and more expensive. The women wore dresses with ruffled sleeves and hats trimmed with flowers, feathers, and colorful ribbons, while many of the men wore suits and felt bowlers instead of cowboy hats.

There were many more children here too. The older ones laughed and played between the buildings or raced along the wooden boards, dodging between the adults, while the younger ones watched with curiosity from their mothers' sides.

Beyond the busy business section of town were rows of stately homes, each surrounded by lush green lawns and wrought-iron fences.

At Third and Grand, they passed a school, and although children played in the shade it offered, it didn't seem to be in session. Grant wondered if it was the weekend or holiday. It was hard keeping track of the days without a calendar or phone. "School's out?"

Butch nodded. "Sure. It's Saturday. No school today. 'Course, this school is for the little ones. There's an upper grade school across town."

"High school?" Ash asked. "I didn't think they had them back then. Er, now. Here. In the west."

"Oh, sure. I expect Laramie's as progressive as Chicago or New York. Well, maybe it's not as grand as either of those cities, but it's a sight bigger than Casper. They got too many students here to have a one-room schoolhouse like in Casper. I hear they got over six thousand people living here now. Imagine that!" Butch said. "They got the railroad to thank for it. The tracks run right past town, and they built a fine station for it. The Union Pacific Hotel and Depot, they call it. Union Pacific brought lots of jobs and money into the area."

He led them to a large shop, the *Trading Commercial Company Store*. They tethered their horses to a rail outside the shop and followed Butch inside.

"Whoa!" Grant pointed to the bright bulbs in fancy fixtures on the walls of the shop and hanging in elaborate chandeliers. "Are those lightbulbs?"

"Yes, sir. Got them electricity just last year. Cost 'em a pretty penny to get it all installed, but the richest houses all have it now, or so folks say." Butch sniffed. "Someday, I'm gonna have a house with electric lights in it. Just you wait and see."

The store was long and wide, well lit by the electric lights, and filled to the rafters with items of every description. Ash thought it looked like Urhman's Cheap Cash Store back in Casper, except on steroids. For example, it didn't offer *one* coffee grinder for sale—it had two dozen of them, in different sizes. Dozens of bolts of colorful material filled an entire corner, along with other sewing notions—spools of thread in a rainbow of color, pins, fancy sewing machines that worked by cranking a handle, spinning wheels, and looms.

Another section of the store was dedicated to hardware. Nuts, bolts, nails in different sizes, all manner of hand tools, hammers, saws, hatchets, axes, shovels, and plowshares. Next came a section devoted to all things cowboy—beautifully tooled leather saddles, horse blankets, bridles, rope, boots, gloves, hats, and every conceivable type of camping gear available at the time.

There were tables of men's clothing, and another of ready-to-wear women's dresses. Silverware, glassware, china, and bric-a-brac filled another set of shelves. Bedding, including thick goose-feather comforters and lace-trimmed pillows, rounded out the stock.

If Urhman's Cheap Cash Store was the Walmart of 1899, Ash thought, then the Trading Commercial Company Store was the Wild West version of Amazon.

Butch led them over to the cowboy section. They quickly spied what he was looking for—a display case stocked with handguns. Each gun had a small, neatly handprinted sign proclaiming its type. There was a shiny Colt .45, which, according to the sign, was also called the Peacemaker, a Remington revolver, a Colt double-action revolver, and a Derringer, which was small enough to fit in Ash's palm.

A rack of rifles was set behind the glass case. Butch pointed out a Springfield Allin Conversion Rifle, a double-barrel shotgun, and one even Ash had heard of—a Winchester.

Butch quickly turned their attention back to the glass case. "Now, let's see here. I think a smaller caliber gun would be better suited to you, considering you're just learnin' and all. Don't want too much kick." He pointed to one. "This Colt double-action is a .38. That ought to do you. Did you know Teddy Roosevelt and his Rough Riders all carried one just like it when they stormed San Juan Hill last year. It's true. I heard it from a man who was there." Butch shrugged. "Or said he was, anyway."

He motioned to the shopkeeper, who'd been waiting to one side, clearly watching the merchandise but trying not to be obvious about it. The man hurried over to the case. Butch pointed to a gun. "How much for the double-action Colt?"

The man smiled. "Oh, that's a fine choice, sir. Well made, and I heard the Rough Riders carried one just like this last year when they took San Juan Hill."

Butch glanced at Ash and Grant and smirked. "See? Told you so."

The shopkeeper continued. "This will set you back twenty-five dollars."

Butch gasped, as if horrified. "That's robbery!"

"Oh, now, sir, I assure you it's not! That's a very fair price for this weapon. If you want something less expensive, I could show you the Derringer. It's small, a .22, but—"

"Do I look like the sort of man who'd want to carry a pissant little gun like that?" Butch growled. His hand slid toward his holster, resting lightly on the butt of his gun.

The shopkeeper visibly paled. "Um, no, sir. I meant no offense. It's just that—"

Butch chuckled. "Aw, I'm just funnin' with you. Look, I want two of these here double-actions. You got two in stock?"

"Yes, sir. Indeed." The shopkeeper chuckled nervously, as if he didn't quite believe Butch was just kidding.

"Good. Now, since I'm fixin' to buy two of these beauties, I think we can come up with a better price, don't you?" Butch raised an eyebrow. It was obvious to anyone watching that he expected the answer to be yes.

The shopkeeper must've dealt with dangerous men on a regular basis, because he agreed immediately. "Oh, um, yes. Yes, of course. How about, er, twenty-two dollars each?"

"Forty for the pair," Butch countered.

"Sir! I'll just break even at that price—"

"Forty. For the pair." Butch didn't phrase it as an offer this time. More like a demand.

The shopkeeper swallowed visibly. "Forty for the pair. It's a deal."

Butch grinned. "Good!" He pulled out his small moneybag from where he kept it looped on his belt and counted out forty dollars. He slid the small pile across the counter to the shopkeeper. As an afterthought, he added another twenty to the stack. "Gonna need ammunition for both guns and a pair of holsters."

The shopkeeper nodded, then hurried off toward the back of the store.

Butch watched him go, then turned to Ash and Grant. "Gotta dicker to get a good price. Remember that, boys. Never give 'em what they ask for right off. They can always do better."

Ash and Grant nodded, but Ash wondered what Butch would think of twenty-first century prices. He didn't know how much a revolver cost in his own time, but he was pretty sure it was a hell of a lot more than twenty bucks. And if you tried to haggle a price in a modern-day department store, you'd get tossed out the doors.

The shopkeeper wasted no time returning with the second Colt, a pair of leather holsters, and four boxes of ammunition. "Got yourself two hundred rounds here." He took the first Colt out of the display case and added it to the pile of merchandise. "You want me to wrap it up?"

"Nah. I expect they'll be wearin' them home." Butch chuckled and jerked his head to indicate Ash and Grant.

"Oh, I see. Buying your boys their first weapons?"

"Something like that." Butch gave a small shrug, then turned to Ash and Grant. "Okay, boys, belts off."

He waited as Ash and Grant fumbled with their belts, then showed them how to attach the holster and position it so it hung comfortably at their side. Then he handed them each a gun, and two boxes of ammunition. "Load your weapons, then put the rest in your saddlebags. Go on, have a look around town. I'll meet you outside in an hour or so. I want to get a few other things while I'm here."

Ash and Grant thanked Butch, then went outside and did as he told them. Once the ammo was secured in their saddlebags, they tried to decide where to go.

"I could use food. I'm hungry." Ash glanced around, then pointed to a restaurant down the street, *Cattlemen Steakhouse.* "How about there?"

"Butch may want to eat too." Grant shook his head. "We ought to wait for him, don't you think?"

"Well, then let's go to the pharmacy over there." Ash pointed in another direction. "At least we can get a soda in the meantime."

They meandered toward the pharmacy, which also boasted a soda fountain according to the gold lettering on the front window, and stepped inside. The shop didn't have electricity, at least not that they could see, but it didn't need electric lights. It was small enough for the bright sunshine outside to illuminate the entire interior.

Like the one in Casper, the pharmacy had shelves of bottles, ointments, pills, and tinctures toward the rear of the store. The front was dominated by a soda fountain, albeit a much larger and fancier one than what they'd seen in Casper. This counter was built from carved wood and had shiny brass trim. A small hand-lettered sign behind it proclaimed sodas to be a nickel each.

A man wearing an apron looked up when they approached the counter. "Help you boys?"

"Yes, sir. What flavors do you have?" Grant asked.

"The usual, chocolate, cherry, and vanilla. We also got a new mix straight from New York City. Called an "egg cream," though why I don't know. Don't have no eggs in it. It's chocolate, cream, and seltzer."

"I'll take one of those." Grant dug out a dime from his pocket.

"I'll have a cherry soda," Ash said. "He's paying."

The soda jerk swiped the dime from the counter and set about making their drinks. To their surprise, the drinks were cold.

Grant's curiosity was piqued. "How do you keep the soda so nice and cold?"

The clerk raised an eyebrow, as if they were stupid. "Ice from the icehouse."

"Oh. Sure. Of course." Grant felt as stupid as the clerk seemed to think he was. He concentrated on drinking his soda. "Oh, wow, this is good."

"Yeah, that's what folks are saying." The clerk walked off to help a woman who'd come in after them. She claimed she suffered from headaches, and Grant heard the clerk suggest something called effervescent brain salts.

He didn't even want to know what ingredients might be in something called brain salts. "Hurry up and finish your soda, Ash. We need to go meet Butch where we left the horses."

Ash drained his glass, slurping the last bits from the bottom. He had a cherry mustache when he was done, and looked so cute Grant had to resist the urge to lick it off. "I'm ready."

Butch was just walking up the street when they got back to their horses, carrying several packages wrapped in brown paper. "Ready to ride, boys? I got me some good cuts of beef and a passel of potatoes and carrots. Gonna make for a real fine stew."

"We're ready, Butch," Grant said as he mounted up, swinging himself up into the saddle as if he'd been born there.

Ash was a little more awkward in mounting, but even he'd improved since they'd arrived at the Hole in the Wall cabin.

Once Butch stored the packages in his saddlebags and mounted his stallion, he led them up the street and out of Laramie.

Grant glanced over his shoulder at the bustling city. It was probably the first and last visit he'd make to Laramie, at least the last time in 1899. If he went back in his own time, it would look vastly different, and he wanted to remember how it looked now so he could make the comparison. It would be interesting to see how much it changed.

Then he turned to look forward again, and they left Laramie behind. He wondered if they'd be able to get the Colt .45 out of the lockbox before he had to ride south again and help the Wild Bunch rob a train.

CHAPTER 15

They camped for the night next to a meandering stream that wasn't much more than a trickle but enough to provide them and their horses with water. Butch built a small fire and roasted a piece of the beef he'd bought in Laramie for their supper.

They each carried a metal plate and utensils along with their bedrolls, and after dinner, they washed them in the stream, then spread out their blankets to bed down for the night. Ash and Grant lay down, rolled up snug in their blankets next to the sputtering fire, looking up at a sky studded with uncountable stars and a big, yellow moon.

"Ever tell you about my very first bank robbery?" Butch sat up, sipping at a cup full of strong coffee he'd brewed earlier in a small metal pot over the campfire. "It was 'round 'bout this time of year, June twenty-fourth, to be exact. This was ten years ago, back in 1889. I met Matt Warner outside of Telluride. He had a racehorse, and I rode it for him. Met the McCarty brothers there. Let's see, there was Tom, of course, the leader of the McCarty gang, and Henry, Bill, Matt, and Bill's son Fred.

"Anyway, me, Matt, and Tom held up the San Miguel Bank in Telluride. Got about twenty thousand dollars for our trouble. First time out, can you believe it?" He laughed. "I tell you what, I was nervous enough to piss my britches the whole time. Good thing I didn't have to shoot anybody during that robbery—I probably would've shot my own damn foot off, I was shaking so hard."

Soft snoring made Grant look back from the velvet diamond-studded sky toward Ash's bedroll. He was out like a light, sleeping with his mouth open, a thin drip of drool snaking from the corner of his mouth.

Butch didn't seem insulted at all that Ash had fallen asleep during his story. Instead, he drained the last of his coffee, said goodnight, then stretched out on his own blanket.

Grant looked back at the sky. It stretched forever in all directions, bright with stars, too many to count. It was so different from the sky in his own time. There were no city lights to compete with the light of the stars, no towering skyscrapers to block out the horizon. The sky seemed huge and made him feel very small in comparison.

He wasn't aware when his eyelids drifted close, but when they opened again, it was morning.

And Ash was gone.

Butch was brewing another pot of coffee. He smiled at Grant and motioned to a frying pan half-full of cornbread. "Help yourself. Coffee will be ready in two shakes."

"Thanks." Grant turned around in a circle. "Where's Ash?"

Butch chuckled. "I ain't never seen a boy so shy about doing his business in sight of anybody. He rode off to find somewhere private. I reckon he'll be back in a few minutes. Lest he gets snakebit."

"Snakes!" Grant had started to sit down next to the fire but stopped halfway, as if a rattler might be curled up at his feet.

Butch shrugged. "Lots of 'em out here. Gotta keep an eye peeled for rattlesnakes."

Grant stood back up. "Maybe I ought to go look for him."

"I don't know where he went. It's a big country out here. You're not likely to find him. Set yourself down and eat some breakfast. He'll be back." Butch didn't seem worried in the slightest, but Butch didn't know Ash like Grant did. He didn't know Ash was a city boy, only recently dumped into the Wild West and who had little to no knowledge of poisonous snakes in Wyoming.

Or wolves.

Or bears.

Or Native Americans who might be less than pleased to find Ash taking a leak on sacred ground.

He was about to press the issue when hoofbeats sounded and he saw a cloud of dust in the distance.

"I reckon that's him now," Butch said.

A figure on horseback loomed out of the dust cloud, and as it drew closer, Grant saw it was, indeed, Ash. He felt a wash of relief as Ash closed the distance and pulled his horse up to a stop near their camp.

"Hey, sleepyhead. I thought for sure you were going to sleep to noon." Ash grinned at Grant as he walked up to them. He sat down and helped himself to a wedge of cornbread. He stuffed half of it into his mouth.

Grant reached over and swatted Ash on the arm. "Where were you? I was just getting ready to ride out to try to find you!"

"Why? I wasn't lost. I needed to find a bathroom."

"That's ridiculous. It's not like you were going to ride across a 7-Eleven in the middle of the prairie! Why didn't you just go here?"

"Since when are you my mother? I go where I want."

"Do you have any idea what could've happened to you out

there? We probably couldn't have found you if we tried, and you could've been bitten by a snake or eaten by a bear or—"

Butch interjected as he poured himself another cup of coffee. "Nah, bears ain't likely to come down from the mountains. You're more likely to get trampled by a buffalo."

Grant gestured toward Butch. "See? You could've got caught in a buffalo stampede."

"There were no buffalo. No snakes either. Come on, Grant, cut me some slack. I'm not an idiot." Ash scowled at him.

"Could've fooled me, riding off by yourself like that, not telling anybody where you were going—"

"You sound like my mother."

Grant growled. "I sound like somebody who was worried about you."

"Boys, boys!" Butch cut in before things could escalate and a punch was thrown. "Calm yourselves and take a seat. If'n you can't control yourselves better than this, I can't risk having you on a job."

That sobered them both. If Butch sent them packing, they'd never get their hands on Merlin's Colt .45!

"Okay, then. Settled down? Good. Pack your horses and mount up. I want to be back at Hole in the Wall before dark." Butch set about following his own order, gathering his utensils and bedroll. Grant and Ash followed suit, both unusually silent.

Grant, for one, was sorry he'd let Ash know how worried he'd been. It wasn't cool. Ash was right—his behavior reeked of a parental unit, not a boyfriend. He felt angry at Ash for going off and not telling him, but at the same time, upset with himself for getting so frantic.

"Hey."

He looked over at Ash. "Yeah?"

"I'm sorry I went off and didn't tell you. I really didn't

plan to go far—just out of sight of camp." Ash actually looked sheepish. "I started walking and thinking about the train robbery and"—he glanced toward Butch—"you know, other stuff, and before I knew it, I was out past the hill there. I started back as soon as I could."

"Nah, it's okay. I shouldn't have got so upset. I'm not your keeper. You can make your own decisions." Grant shrugged. He felt his mood lighten though. He really didn't like fighting with Ash. In the past, they had to depend on each other if they wanted to get back home. Plus, he really did have feelings for Ash. He just needed to sort them out.

It was…complicated. He was attracted to Ash, without question. Ash was good-looking, cool, and while he was often a pain in Grant's posterior, he also could always be counted on making Grant laugh. There was a vulnerable side to Ash, too, one he tried to keep hidden, but that Grant got a peek at now and then. It was the kid who got ignored at home, whose folks had issues with booze and with a son who identified as gay. The kid who, like himself, rebelled and got into trouble with the law. The one who lashed out from time to time, unable to process his own feelings.

Grant grunted and sighed, a little embarrassed and disgusted with himself. He needed to stop watching those touchy-feely daytime talk shows, like *Dr. Phil*. They were screwing with his brain. Next thing he knew, he'd be wanting to go to couples' therapy with Ash to sort through their issues. Yuck.

Turning his attention back to the task at hand, he finished rolling up his bedding and packing his horse. Then he mounted up and waited for Ash and Butch to finish. He struggled to keep his mind on the journey back to Hole in the Wall, but the hours on horseback, riding through a monochrome prairie, encouraged his mind to wander.

And unfortunately, it kept wandering back to Ash and

how Grant felt about him. Above all else remained the nagging question of whether or not Ash felt the same way.

* * *

WHEN THEY ARRIVED BACK at Hole in the Wall, the rest of the gang was already there, waiting for them. Etta took the meat and potatoes Butch brought with him, and set about putting together a stew that shortly filled the cabin with a mouthwatering aroma, reminding Grant and Ash how hungry they were. They hadn't eaten anything since breakfast except for a couple of strips of leathery beef jerky, which they'd chewed while riding. Butch hadn't wanted to stop for lunch; they stopped only long enough to water the horses on the way back.

Kid, Lonnie, and Johnny Curry had been to Kemmerer, a town about two hundred and fifty miles west of Hole in the Wall, where they purchased five hundred rounds of ammunition. Meanwhile, Will Carver and Flat Nose had gone back to Casper and stolen a crate of dynamite from the mine at Eadsville.

The crate made Grant nervous, and he was glad it was left outside the cabin, near the far side of the corral under a little wooden lean-to. He'd hate to think of what might happen to anything nearby if it blew.

For sure, it would be very, very messy. Wood splinters and horse parts everywhere. He shuddered and hoped he and Ash wouldn't be anywhere near it if it exploded.

Nobody mentioned the robbery until after dinner. After Butch scraped the last bite of stew from his bowl, he belched, then pushed his bowl away. "Okay. We're all set then? Everybody understand the plan?"

Everyone nodded or grunted in assent. No one, Grant and Ash included, asked any questions.

Butch propped his booted feet up on the table. "Good. Today is the twenty-fifth of May. You'll leave at dawn tomorrow, make the ride down to Wilcox. Camp out there. June the second, we hit the train. Then we meet up back here."

Everyone grunted again, each busy either eating or cleaning a weapon. Three men sat on the floor near the stove, playing cards. Nobody seemed overly nervous about the upcoming robbery.

Nobody except Grant and probably Ash. Grant felt his stomach twisted into knots with worry. What if something went wrong? What if the dynamite blew on the way to Wilcox? What if the law found out about the robbery and caught them? How would he and Ash ever get home if they were locked up in prison in 1899?

He was never going to be able to sleep. Not a wink.

Later that night, he lay in his bedroll outside the cabin. It was a beautiful night, the sky glimmering with a myriad of sparkling stars, the breeze warm, and they'd opted to sleep outside rather than on the floor of the cabin.

"You nervous?" Ash whispered to him. They'd laid out their bedrolls far enough from the cabin that it was unlikely anyone would overhear a hushed conversation between them.

"Yes. A lot. Anything could go wrong, Ash. We could get shot. Or blown up. Or arrested. Or—"

"Shush. It's gonna be fine, Grant. We know from history that the train robbery took place. We also know from Merlin that we can't change events in the past. Remember?"

Grant took in a deep, calming breath. "I know; you're right. But just because the train gets robbed doesn't mean we can't get blown up in the process."

"We won't." Ash chuckled. "It'll be fine. I'm looking forward to it. I mean, when does anybody get the chance to be a real-life Wild West outlaw?"

Grant snorted. "Leave it to you to get excited about possibly ending up as bits of kid confetti."

"We'll be fine. Now, go to sleep. It'll be morning before we know it, and we've got a long ride tomorrow."

"Yes, mom."

"Shut up." Grant could hear the amusement in Ash's reply to his sarcasm, and smiled to himself, but he was unable to shake off his case of nerves. He tucked his arms under his head and gazed at the sky, sure he wouldn't sleep a wink.

The next thing he knew, Ash was shaking him awake. "Time to rise and shine, Sleeping Beauty."

He blinked against the early-morning light. The sky was just coloring pink with sunrise and the air already warming. He groaned and sat up and then rubbed the sleep from his eyes. "You know, when we get back, the first thing I'm going to do is sleep for about forty-eight hours."

"Sure, sure. Whatevs. For now, you need to get up. We're riding down to Wilcox today."

"I know, I know." He stretched, then dragged himself to his feet. "Gonna go pee. Then I need coffee."

"Hurry up, boys. I thought maybe you were going to sleep until noon." Butch called to them from the front door of the cabin. "Etta's got breakfast ready, and you boys need to get on the trail afore long."

Grant pushed himself to move and wandered off a bit into the brush to do his morning business. When he returned, the gang was sitting either at the small table or on the floor or cabin porch, eating some sort of hash and corn-bread. He joined Ash at the stove and helped himself to a cup of coffee.

He took a sip and grimaced. It tasted strong enough to dissolve steel. There was no alternative though. Mocha lattes would not be available for another hundred years.

Etta scooped some hash onto a flat metal plate, added a

slice of cornbread, and handed it to him. He murmured a thanks, then followed Ash outside to the porch. They sat with their backs against the cabin wall to eat.

The hash was hearty, a mix of sausage and potatoes. It was the sort of breakfast that would stick to the ribs, and the cornbread, while a bit dry, was tasty. Etta wasn't a half-bad cook, Grant decided. He ate it all, then walked his plate over to a rain barrel filled with water and washed it. He returned it to Etta, along with the mug he'd used for his coffee.

"All right, boys. Mount up! It's time," Butch called out, clapping his hands to get everyone's attention like a school-teacher with a roomful of rowdy students.

None of the Wild Bunch looked even vaguely amused. They got to their feet and went about their business of saddling and packing their horses, taking their time and occasionally shooting Butch an irritated glance.

Grant and Ash mounted their horses. Grant was feeling anxious and his stomach churned, making him wonder if having breakfast was such a great idea after all. All he could think of were the things that could go wrong with Butch's plan and how any of those things could keep him and Ash from ever going back home. They could be shot during the holdup. They could be arrested. Hell, one of them could be thrown from his horse and crack his head open on a boulder. Or get snakebit. The possibilities were endless, and all of them bad.

Ash, however, just looked excited. He was grinning, and his eyes positively sparkled. Grant understood why—this was Ash's fantasy, playing outlaw, riding with a group of famous bandits, going to rob a train. He had a gun on his hip and a cowboy hat on his head. For Ash, Grant realized, it didn't get better than this. Grant was positive there wasn't a single negative thought going through Ash's brain.

He admitted he was a little jealous of Ash's ability to

ignore the dangers and concentrate on the fantasy. Ash was like a little kid in that regard, playing cowboy, innocent of any hazard.

"Hai!" Sundance called out and spurred his horse forward. The rest of the gang followed in a loose line. Ash and Grant pulled up the rear.

It would take them a couple of days to ride down to Wilcox but less time coming back since they planned to hard ride all the way to Hole in the Wall after the robbery. That's why Butch planned to have fresh horses waiting for them at the prearranged place. Coming back, they wouldn't sleep until they reached the cabin again. Day and night, riding hard. It would be exhausting, and Grant wasn't looking forward to it.

He didn't have much of a choice. In fact, he had no choice at all. If he and Ash backed out now, Butch would never let them have the Colt .45. In fact, he doubted if Butch—or at least Sundance or Kid Curry—would let them live. They'd get a bullet in the head and a shallow grave for their trouble.

No, he was going to have to see the robbery through. But when they got back to the cabin, he and Ash were going to need to come up with a way to get the lockbox from under the bed. A plan was already formulating in his head.

Butch didn't seem to carry the lockbox with him. It was under the bed when they arrived at the cabin, after all. He must leave it there for safekeeping. If so, all he and Ash had to do was wait until the rest of the gang cleared out after splitting up their take from the robbery, then break into the cabin and steal the lockbox.

They'd just need to smash the lock to get at the Colt, and then Merlin's magic would whisk them home.

Easy peasy, lemon squeezy, as his grandma used to say.

So, all they had to do was survive the trip and the robbery and make it back to Hole in the Wall.

CHAPTER 16

They took two days on the trail riding to Wilcox, skirting the sparsely populated area in favor of a remote one, sheltered by a tall, rough red bluff. They'd been very careful not to be seen, taking every precaution to remain invisible, not even lighting campfires at night. They ate cold lunches put up for them by Etta, and chewed on strips of leathery beef jerky. All they drank was water from their canteens or from a clear-running brook when they came across one.

It wasn't exactly a party trip.

There was no joking, no laughing, no kidding around between them. Every one of the them was somber, quiet, and prone to snarl if annoyed. Ash realized the men were focused; they meant business. This trip wasn't fun for them —it was work. The Wild Bunch were deadly earnest about it, refusing to indulge in the simplest of conveniences if it might, however remotely, swing the eye of the law toward them. They were thieves, but professional ones, and they acted like it.

Ash felt he was getting a good idea now of exactly what

the life of an outlaw in the Wild West was like, and it wasn't anything like what he'd seen on television and the movies. There were very few days spent gambling and drinking and cutting up in saloons, and almost none of shooting up towns for the sport of it. There were, however, lots of days spent sitting around, chewing straw, smoking gross-smelling cheroots, drinking turpentine whiskey, and fooling around with women who looked worn, tired, and faded. If anyone was gay here, other than himself and Grant, they were so deep in the closet he doubted they could even see the door.

He was pretty much over being in the wild Wild West. His mouth was caked with trail dust, and his butt ached from being in the saddle. He wanted to go home. Back to luxuries he usually took for granted, like hot and cold running water, electric lights, refrigerators full of icy Cokes, microwaves, and television. Beds with genuine mattresses and hypoallergenic pillows. Nintendo, Xbox, and PlayStation. Movies with tubs of hot buttered popcorn and extra-large fountain drinks. Where he could be himself without worrying about somebody stringing him up by the neck because he loved another guy.

Hell, he even missed school.

Feeling morose, his mouth set in a grim line. He rode along without speaking, not even to Grant. Every passing mile saw him sink deeper into a funk. Why did he always think the past was such a fun place? Why did he always believe what he'd read in history books or seen on television? The reality was never anything half as nice as what was portrayed.

Things in the past *always* smelled bad. Everything smelled of body odor, animal poop, and smoke. There was never enough heat, enough light, enough food, enough water, enough *anything*. Everyday chores were hard enough to raise blisters, and you went to bed at night exhausted, stretched out on a hard pallet or on the ground, muscles aching from the amount of work necessary to just survive.

It sucked. It *always* sucked.

"You look like you swallowed a groundhog ass-end first."

He startled and looked up to see Sundance riding next to him. Sundance had a kerchief pulled up over his mouth and nose to keep from breathing in too much trail dust, but his dark blue eyes were unmistakable, and their penetrating stare was focused on Ash.

He shrugged. "Just tired of riding. Want this trip to be over."

Sundance smirked at him. "Anxious to get to the train, huh? I remember my first train robbery. I was so excited I practically shit my trousers."

"Not really. I'm sick of eating trail dust all day long."

"Well, for corn's sake, son. Tie on a kerchief. Keep the dust out of your lungs." Sundance clucked his tongue and shook his head. "I swear, you young 'uns don't have the sense God gave a tadpole. I got to tell you, I was against Butch signing you two on. You got the look of greenhorns on you, and the last thing we need is a couple of kids who don't know their butts from their elbows messing things up."

"We're not kids!" They were, of course, but Ash wasn't in the mood to be agreeable. "We know what we're doing."

"Sure you do. That's why you've been breathing in enough sand to puke up a desert, when you got a perfectly good handkerchief tied around your neck." Sundance scoffed, his disbelief evident in his sarcastic tone. "Look, for better or worse, you and your friend are part of this gang. You're what folks call *probationary* members though. How's that for a ten-dollar word? Means you better obey everything we tell you, do your job, and not screw up, or you'll find yourself drummed out of the gang—or left to rot someplace in the desert. Got it?"

"Yeah, I got it." Ash frowned. He pulled up his kerchief over his mouth and nose, the thin material serving to filter out the worst of the trail dust. It also seemed to function as a conversation ender, since Sundance clucked his tongue and rode on ahead without another word.

A few moments later, Grant rode up next to him. "What did Sundance want?"

Ash was still feeling grumpy, and his conversation with Sundance hadn't helped his mood at all. "Nothing. Just giving me a friendly reminder that we're kids, don't know our asses from our elbows, and how we better do as we're told and not screw up." He left out the implied death threat Sundance had tacked on. No sense in getting Grant worked up. It'd only make things worse than they already were.

Grant grunted. "Great. Adults are the same in every time period, aren't they? None of them ever give anybody under thirty credit for having half a brain."

"He acts like we can't follow simple directions. Made sure to remind me we're not *real* members of the gang."

Grant shrugged. "Well, I'm not defending him, but technically, we're not. I mean, Butch took us in and included us in the plan to rob the train, but we're not *really* members of the Wild Bunch."

Ash shot him a gloomy look. "Whose side are you on?"

"The fact is, we're not outlaws, Ash. We're a couple of high school kids from the future, remember?"

"That doesn't mean we aren't capable of pulling our weight as members of the gang."

One sleek eyebrow cocked in an expression of amusement Ash had often seen on Grant's face. "Do you even hear yourself talk? Listen carefully—we aren't outlaws. We don't break the law."

Ash snorted. "Yes, we do. That's how we both got sent to

Stanton's School for Boys, remember? I boosted a car, and you broke into your dad's offices."

Grant rolled his eyes. "Okay, okay. Correction. We don't break the law *anymore*."

Ash answered with a low growl in his throat and a tap of his heels to his horse's sides, which urged the beast into a trot. His brief conversation with Grant had only irritated him and left his mood even more sour.

Grant caught up to him easily though. "What the hell is wrong with you? What did I say wrong?"

"Nothing." His back teeth clenched hard enough to hurt, and his forehead scrunched into a fierce frown.

"Oh? Because you look like you're ready to kill somebody. Namely, me, and I don't even know what I did wrong."

Ash shot him a black look. "I'm not the one threatening to kill people."

Grant sat back on his mount, his expression crumpling into a frown that matched Ash's. "What are you talking about? Who threatened to kill someone?"

"Sundance, just now. He said that if we screwed up, we could find ourselves left to rot in the desert. What else is that supposed to mean?"

"Wow." Grant's gaze shifted toward Sundance, who was riding at the head of the loose formation of outlaws. After a minute, he looked back at Ash. "Well, we won't screw up. And we have each other's backs, right? I mean, I have yours. They'd have to go through me to get to you."

Ash nodded and summoned up a small smile. "Yeah, well, I don't think you'd make much of a roadblock for a bullet, but I appreciate the sentiment."

"I would totally take a bullet for you."

Ash felt his bad mood dissipate and grinned. "Let's hope it doesn't come to that. I don't want to have to explain why I brought you home looking like Swiss cheese."

"Hey, I said *a* bullet. One. Single. Let's not get carried away."

Ash laughed. He looked ahead. The rest of the Wild Bunch had ridden far ahead of them. "Heard. Come on. If we don't get a move on, we're going to get left behind, and we'll never get home, holey or otherwise."

* * *

THE TRAIN WAS due to hit the tracks in front of them in just under two days. That gave them plenty of time to go over the plan again, for Flat Nose and Will to set the charges under the bridge, and for Grant to become absolutely neurotic with worry.

"What if something goes wrong with the dynamite charges? What if somebody gets hurt? Or worse, killed? I don't want to be a murderer, Ash." Grant wrung his hands and paced, his feet kicking up little puffs of desert sand.

They'd gone for a walk and were out of earshot of the rest of the gang. It'd been Ash's idea—he'd seen how Grant was fixing to roll headfirst into Crazy Town, obsessing over the plan and every way it could possibly go wrong, and figured they'd need some privacy. The last thing they needed was for Sundance or one of the others to realize Grant was stepping off the deep end into a pool of paranoia and send them back to Butch.

Or worse, decide he and Grant were a danger to the plan and the gang, and shoot them both. He wouldn't put it past Kid Curry to think killing them would be the easiest solution to the problem. Kid was, in Ash's opinion, the most dangerous and unpredictable of the Wild Bunch. Kid bragged about how many men he'd killed the way kids back home bragged about how many Pokémon characters they'd captured.

"Nothing is going to go wrong, Grant. You need to calm your ass down." Ash grabbed Grant's arm and pulled him to a stop. All the pacing was making him nervous, and *one* of them had to keep a cool head. "Butch wouldn't have sent us on this job if there was a chance of it going bad."

Grant scowled. "How do you know that? He's not here, is he? He stayed behind where it's safe! If anything goes wrong, he's miles away!"

"He stayed behind because if he were to get caught pulling this job, he'd be sent back to prison for the rest of his life or hung."

"So, if we get caught, it's okay?"

"We're not going to get caught! We're not even going to be here when the robbery goes down, remember? We're going to be on the other side of the bridge when it blows. We stop the second train, that's all. Even if we're caught, we can just say we were trying to save the people on the second train because we saw the bridge was out."

Grant continued to glower, but Ash could see his mind working behind the fierce expression. Finally, he seemed to —grudgingly—relax a little. "Yeah, I guess that makes sense."

"Of course it does! Now, come on. I want to watch Flat Nose and Will set the charges."

"Why?"

"Because I've only seen it done in the movies. That's why."

"Yeah, well, I've only ever seen a zombie apocalypse in the movies, but I have no ambition to experience one in real life!"

Ash growled and grabbed Grant's hand, pulling him along. "Come on. Enough crazy for one day, okay?"

Grant plodded along behind him, muttering under his breath all the way. "Gonna get blown up. I just know it. Gonna have my bits and pieces scattered from here to Albuquerque."

They reached the camp just as Flat Nose and Will were getting ready to carry the box of dynamite to the bridge. The words *Safety Nitro Powder Company*, Dynamite, and the address of the company in San Francisco were printed in fancy scrolled lettering on the side of the crate. Ash and Grant followed along behind the two men—at a safe distance. As much as Ash thought Grant was paranoid about possible explosions, he agreed it was better to be safe than blown to smithereens.

The bridge was a wooden trestle bridge, old-fashioned and picturesque, like something you'd see in an old-timey movie. It was wide enough only for the train to chug its way over the sluggish river below. Ash and Grant sat on the bank of the river, watching Flat Nose and Will go to work setting the charges.

Flat Nose and Will set the crate down on the mossy riverbank just under the trestle bridge. Flat Nose used a crowbar to pry up the lid of the crate. Inside, nestled in a thick padding of straw, were red paper-wrapped sticks of dynamite. Ash was surprised to see they looked almost identical to the sticks used by Wile E. Coyote in the old Roadrunner cartoons he'd watched as a kid.

The men seemed to use extreme caution in handling the sticks—and with good reason, Ash realized. They really had no idea how old the dynamite was since they'd stolen it from the abandoned mine. Dynamite tended to sweat nitroglycerin when it aged, making the sticks exceedingly unstable. One might explode for no reason other than being bumped against the ground or handled too roughly. Flat Nose or Will could be killed at worst, or seriously injured at best if that happened.

Will and Flat Nose carefully bundled several sticks together and secured them with coarse string. Once they had two bundles prepared, Flat Nose scaled the trestle's wooden support structure until he was just under the tracks. Will followed, handing him a bundle of dynamite sticks. Working quickly but with a steadier hand than Ash would've thought possible considering the potentially deadly consequences should one of the sticks explode prematurely, Flat Nose attached the bundle to the support structure. Only after he'd repeated the process with the second bundle on the other side of the bridge, did they all breathe a sigh of relief.

Both bundles trailed a very long length of cotton cord over the riverbank, which would serve as a fuse. Will could light it from a safe distance, then have a few moments to run even farther before the lit fuse ignited the dynamite and the bridge blew skyward.

The two outlaws, their job done, headed back to camp, but Ash and Grant remained behind. They sat on the river-bank, watching the lazy river meander past. Every so often, Ash would glance at the bridge. It had appeared so quaint before, but now it seemed ominous since he knew two deadly dynamite charges were strapped underneath it.

"You know, this is the first time we're actually breaking the law. I mean, since we started at the Stanton School."

Ash turned to look at Grant. "I know. It's sort of both-ering me too. I mean, can we justify doing something we know is wrong just to fix a mistake we made?"

Grant shrugged. "I don't know. They'd rob the train anyway, whether we were here or not. It's history, and we can't change it. Merlin's magic won't allow it. But does it make us bad people to help pull off a crime that's going to happen whether we want it to or not?"

"And does it matter that we're not really going to rob the train. We're just going to stop the second train from going over the bridge and into the river. Technically, we're saving people."

"But we wouldn't have to save them if the Wild Bunch

weren't going to blow up the bridge to rob the train in the first place."

Ash groaned and lay back against the soft moss-covered bank. He tucked his hands under his head and stared up at a clear, blue sky. "Thinking about this is giving me a headache."

Grant flopped down next to him. "Yeah, me too. And it doesn't matter anyway. We have to do it. If we backed out now, none of the Wild Bunch would trust us. Cassidy would be pissed at us, and he'd never give us his gun."

"What makes you think he'll give it to us even if we help rob the train?"

Grant blinked at him. "Well... I mean, of course... He has to! We need it to go home!"

"I know that, but he doesn't, and if we told him, he'd never believe us. He'd think we were nuts."

They fell silent, both thinking, trying to sort out the problem. Then a thought struck Ash.

"Oh, hey! I think I've got it. After the robbery, the guys will all have money, right?"

"Yeah, so?"

Ash grinned. "What do outlaws do when they have money?"

Grant frowned, then brightened. "They spend it! In town, at the saloon and brothels."

"Exactly! So, all we have to do is wait until Butch and rest of the Wild Bunch go to town. Then we sneak back into the cabin, grab Butch's gun, and we can go home. Easy peasy." He grinned, smugly satisfied that he'd solved their problem.

"What about Etta?"

A slight frown creased Ash's brow. "What about her?"

"She doesn't go to town when the boys go to gamble, does she?"

"I don't know. Maybe. Or maybe Sundance will take her someplace for a nice dinner and shopping or something."

Grant nodded slowly. "Maybe we should suggest it to him, in case he doesn't think of it himself. And pray he thinks it's a good idea, because there's no way we can grab Butch's gun with Etta in the cabin."

"Even if she stays behind, she has to leave the cabin sometime. To work in the garden or feed the animals or collect the eggs from the chickens or hang wash. When she does, we grab the gun and go."

"Don't forget she's a dead shot. I don't want to go through all of this only to get shot by Etta. This plan sounds iffy at best."

Ash sat up, resting one arm on a bent knee, and looked down at Grant. "Yeah, well, right now, iffy is the best we've got. Now, come on, outlaw. We'd better get back before Sundance sends somebody to look for us."

CHAPTER 17

D awn found all the men awake. All of them were in keyed-up moods, excited that the day of the train robbery was finally here. Lonnie and Kid Curry were swigging whiskey from a bottle even though the sun had barely breached the horizon, celebrating as if they'd already completed the robbery and had the money in their pockets. Sundance warned them not to get drunk and fuck up the robbery or he'd put a bullet in each of their heads. Grant had absolutely no doubt Sundance would do exactly as he threatened.

Lonnie and Kid Curry must've believed it, too, because the whiskey bottle disappeared into one of their saddlebags.

For breakfast, they had more of the tough strips of jerky they'd been eating since leaving the cabin a few days ago, and some stale, hard-as-rocks biscuits Etta had baked before they left. None of it was more than barely edible, but it was all they had since Sundance steadfastly refused to allow them to light a campfire.

"We ain't taking no chances on somebody seeing the smoke from a fire and knowing we're here," he said when some of the men complained. "Last thing we need is for some lawman to see it and wonder what folks are doing out here by the tracks. Or worse, have a party of Sioux warriors come riding down on us, thinking we're settlers and easy pickings."

Grant chewed a strip of leathery jerky, hoping it would calm the hunger pangs in his rumbling belly and wishing there was an IHOP nearby. He figured he'd give his left arm for a stack of pancakes smothered in butter and syrup.

"You ready for today?" Ash asked. He was gnawing on a stale biscuit, alternating bites with swallows of water from his canteen.

"I guess so. You?"

"As I can be. When will we go across the bridge?"

"Right after we finish eating, I think I heard Sundance say. I guess it's better to be early than late." Grant looked at the remaining strip of jerky in his hand and tossed it away. "I can't eat anymore of this stuff, anyway. It's going to break my damn teeth."

Ash nodded and discarded what little remained of his biscuit. "Yeah. You know, I would kill for an Egg McMuffin right about now."

Grant chuckled. "I was just thinking basically the same thing, except about pancakes from IHOP."

"Ooh, pancakes. Yes! With lots of butter and maple syrup. And an order of crispy bacon. And breakfast sausage. Four links worth. And hash browns with cheese. And—"

"Okay, okay, I get it! Enough, before you make me so hungry, I start gnawing my own arm off." Grant laughed and stood up. He gestured for Ash to follow him, then walked over to where Sundance was lying down, his hat covering his face. "Hey, Sundance. We're going to head across the bridge to the other side. We want to be ready to do our part."

Sundance lifted the brim of his hat and peeked out at them. "Good. Keep an eye out. And don't mess up if you want

163

to live to see tomorrow morning. The rest of us will be along directly." He let his hat fall back over his face, ending the conversation.

Ash and Grant exchanged an uneasy expression. Grant hoped they didn't screw it up. He had no doubt Sundance would do exactly as promised, and had no ambition to end his life in 1899, left to rot on the plains of Wyoming, picked over by crows and coyotes.

They rode their horses single file across the bridge. It was narrow, no more than a support for the train tracks to span the river below. There was no room to walk except directly over the tracks, and while there was no train scheduled to come for several hours yet, Grant was still nervous and happy to hurry across to the other side. If a train had come, the only place they could go to get out of its way would be to dive over the side into the river. Considering how deep the gorge was, and how shallow the water, it was good bet they'd die either way.

Once Ash and Grant crossed over, they rode their horses up and over a hill, then dismounted and tethered the horses to a fallen log where they'd be out of sight.

"Where should we wait?" Ash was looking around at the landscape on this side of the bridge. It was very similar to the other side—the only difference was in the details.

Grant glanced around. He pointed to a cluster of large boulders off to one side of the tracks. "How about behind those?"

Ash nodded. "That'll work." He led Grant to the boulders, and they settled down in the shade of the boulders, hidden from sight. A glance toward the bridge showed Grant no one on that side could see him and Ash either.

The space wasn't large. They sat side by side, thigh to thigh. Grant could feel Ash's body heat seep through their clothing, warming parts of him in a way the sun's heat could never do. He cleared his throat. "You know, we're really well hidden back here."

"Yup."

"We've got time before the train is due."

"Yup again."

"So, what do you want to do to pass the time?"

Ash turned toward Grant, one eyebrow cocked. "I don't know. You have something in mind?"

Grant grinned. "I can think of one or two things."

Ash returned Grant's smile in kind. An excited heat sparkled in his eyes. "Oh?"

"Yup." He reached for Ash's face, tracing his thumb over the sharp edge of Ash's jawline. He let his finger brush over Ash's lips, then leaned in and pressed their mouths together.

He kept the kiss soft, easy, not pushing. They had time and plenty of it. He intended to savor every minute of the rare private time he had with Ash.

Ash threaded his fingers into Grant's hair and kissed him back. He moaned softly, although the sound was muffled with their lips pressed together.

Grant slipped his fingers between the buttons on Ash's shirt, feeling warm skin. He'd just started to unbutton the top couple of buttons when a sound pierced the air and broke them apart as easily and quickly as if a bucket of ice water had been thrown over them.

Hoofbeats. The rest of the gang were riding across the bridge. Since the last thing Ash and Grant wanted was to be found by Sundance or Kid Curry in a fierce lip-lock, they broke apart.

Then another sound reached them, and they heard the men on the other side of the boulders swear.

It was a train whistle.

"The train's coming early!" Ash said as they scrambled to their feet. He was buttoning the button Grant had just freed.

"Damn it! I hope everyone is ready for this!" Grant put his hand on Ash's arm. "Remember, we need to stay out of sight until they get the train over the bridge. Our job doesn't start until the second train gets here."

"I know, I know!" Ash's eyes looked a little wild. Adrenaline was probably pumping through him, just as it was with Grant.

The whistle came again, closer this time. They peeked over the top of the boulder, and saw a black engine, gray smoke pouring from its smokestack, approaching from a distance.

The shrill squeal of brakes split the silence. Sundance and the others must have stopped the train by waving lanterns across the tracks. There was shouting and the sound of hoofbeats. A gunshot brought a gasp from Ash's lips. "They're not supposed to kill anybody. Butch said—"

"Shh." Grant put a hand over Ash's mouth. "Quiet. It was probably only a warning shot."

Ash nodded, but he didn't seem fully convinced. They had no more time to discuss it, though, because the train started moving again. In a few moments, it passed by their hiding spot and rumbled across the bridge.

"Alright. They must've boarded the train okay. It's on the other side of the chasm. Get ready. They're going to blow the bridge any min—"

Grant's voice was cut off as a booming blast rocked the ground under their feet. To their left, the bridge exploded into a shower of wood. Sharp splinters fell around them like jagged spears. Ash and Grant dropped behind the boulders again, ducking down and covering their heads with their arms.

When the dust finally settled, they tentatively stood up and looked over at the bridge.

It wasn't completely destroyed, but it might as well have

been. Metal tracks, warped and twisted beyond recognition, hung over the side like a broken arm, deformed by the power of the detonation. Black smoke drifted into the sky, to be scattered by the wind.

"Jeez." Ash's voice was soft and sounded suspiciously like awe.

"Yeah." Grant knew just how he felt. How much dynamite had Flat Nose used under the bridge? It had not only made the bridge unpassable—it almost completely annihilated it.

"Now what?"

Grant looked in the direction the train had come. "Now we wait for the next train. We should light the lanterns. If the first train was early, the second one may be too."

Suddenly, there was a second explosion. They both nearly jumped out of their skins.

"What the hell was that?" Ash craned his neck, trying to see past the boulders.

Grant risked exposure and ran from behind the boulders and to the edge of the chasm where the bridge once stood. Several yards down the track, the first train sat. A black plume of smoke curled into the sky over the first car after the engine. It was too far to see much, but it looked like something must've exploded over there.

"What should we do?" Ash had followed Grant to the edge of the precipice. "Should we run?"

Grant shook his head. "No. We don't know what's going on over there, but we have to be able to tell Butch we did our part."

No sooner had he said it, but another explosion made them jump. Before they could recover from their shock, yet another explosion rent the air.

"Alright, now I'm about to wet my freaking pants. Something must be wrong. Four explosions weren't in the plans."

"I know, but maybe they had to make changes on the spot."

"Or maybe the train was booby-trapped. It could happen. Maybe word got out that the Wild Bunch was looking to rob it, and the railroad set it to blow."

"Doesn't matter. We still stay here and finish our job. If we don't, whoever's on the second train is going to die when the train hits that bridge."

"And if the law shows up?"

"Then we run."

"Right. Like either of us could outride anybody." Ash shook his head. "We'd be screwed."

A whistle sounded and interrupted their argument. Grant had been correct—the second train was early too. There was no more room for discussion—they had to do their part.

He quickly ran to fetch the oil lantern and matches, and worked to light the fuses. He handed one to Ash. "Ready?"

Ash nodded. "Well, at least we don't have to outrun the law—just whoever might be on this train."

Grant gave him a swift smile. "Let's go."

They hurried to the tracks and started running in the direction the train would come. They needed to give the train time and distance enough to stop before hitting the gorge. They stopped about a hundred and twenty yards—the length of a football field—from where they'd hidden behind the boulders. Standing side by side on the tracks, they waited anxiously until they finally saw the engine in the far distance.

Raising their arms, they began waving the lanterns in slow arcs. As the train neared, they heard the unmistakable squeal of brakes. The engineer had seen them and was applying the brakes! Butch's plan was working!

The train coasted to a stop several yards ahead of them. They ran toward the engine.

A man appeared in the open doorway of the engine's cab.

He was older, grizzled, and wore a pair of oil-stained over-alls. "What in tarnation is going on?"

"The bridge is out, mister! You keep going and the train will fall into the gorge!" Grant pointed toward where the bridge had stood.

"He's right. We come from Wilcox. There was some sort of fire. We saw the smoke and came to investigate. Had to climb down to the river, wade across, and climb back up this side."

The old man looked stricken. "The other train! Did the other train make it past?"

"Yes, sir. Made it to Wilcox." Grant offered the man what he hoped was a reassuring smile. The lies he and Ash had to tell the poor old guy were making him feel twitchy though.

"What in hell could make a bridge blow up? Reckon it's bandits? Don't have nothing on this train worth stealing. Money's on the first train. We're just hauling supplies." The engineer drew a handkerchief from his pocket and swiped it over his face.

Ash shrugged. "Don't know. What'll you do now? I mean, now that you can't go forward?"

"Back it up and hope we have enough coal to make it back to Cheyenne." The engineer groaned. "Oh, this is a helluva mess, ain't it?" He looked at Grant and Ash. "Listen, you boys head back to Wilcox, and you get somebody to go on to Medicine Bow. They got them a telegraph there. Make them send a telegram ahead to the railroad, tell 'em what happened. I'm sure Sal—he's running the first engine —will have done it already, but just in case he hasn't, you do it."

"Sure, mister. We'll take care of it."

"Okay. Guess we better get going. Burning coal is wasting coal." He nodded to Grant and Ash and hurried back toward the engine. Another man was walking toward him, but he gestured for the man to get back in the car. "Go on back, George. The bridge is out. We got to backtrack to Cheyenne."

The two men climbed back onto the train, and it slowly began moving backward. Ash and Grant waited until the train was out of sight again before dousing their lanterns and abandoning them behind the boulders. Looking at each other, they broke out into laughter.

Ash snorted. "We're train robbers!"

"Not something we're going to want to put on our resumés, but yeah. We are. By association, anyway." Grant chuckled. "I felt sort of bad lying to the old guy though. I mean, he was only doing his job."

"Yeah, but if we didn't stop him, he would've driven the train into the gorge and he'd be dead. So would the other guy and whoever else is on that train."

"True, true." Grant nodded. "Okay, so now we start riding. Butch said to go due north, and we'd find our way back to Hole in the Wall."

"I remember. Keep the morning sun on our right, and the afternoon sun on our left."

"That's it. Due north."

"What if we get captured by the law?"

"Technically, we didn't do anything wrong. In fact, we're heroes. We saved the second train."

Ash chuckled. "I like the way you think. Okay. Let's get going. I think we should put as many miles between us and these tracks as we can before dark."

CHAPTER 18

Ash didn't think they'd ever get back to Hole in the Wall.

Two day solid of riding with only short breaks to rest and water the horses and a bad night sleeping outside on the cold, hard ground had put him in a foul mood. He wanted to get off his horse. He wanted a bath. He wanted a hot meal. And more than anything, he wanted to go home. As much as he used to love the idea of being a cowboy or an outlaw in the Wild West, actually *being* one sucked. Or, at least, it did at the moment.

It was nearing sunset on the second day when they finally spotted the familiar orange-red bluffs that marked Hole in the Wall.

Ash gave an excited hoot. "There it is! We're almost there!"

"Hush up! If there are any lawmen around, you'll give us away before we have a chance to get down to the cabin!"

They followed the trail down the side of the bluff toward the valley nestling Butch's cabin. Both of them drew their horses up at the sight of a man pointing a shotgun at them.

Grant called out. "Don't shoot, Butch! It's us, Grant and Ash!"

The man lowered his weapon and yelled to them. "Well, what the hell took you so long? Get your butts down here. We got a tale to tell!"

Ash and Grant exchanged a puzzled look, then spurred their horses on. The sooner they made their way down the bluff, the quicker they'd find out what Butch was so excited about. They rode their horses directly to the corral next to the barn, stopping only long enough to unsaddle them and turn them loose to graze.

Inside, only Butch, Sundance, and Etta were waiting. The three of them sat at the table, sipping coffee. When Ash and Grant entered the cabin, Etta got up to serve them dinner.

The cabin was filled with the savory smell of beef stew, which Etta had cooked, and the warm scent of fresh baked bread. She ladled them each a bowlful and topped each plate with a thick slice of bread and fresh-churned butter.

They sat on the floor to eat, but Grant was more curious than hungry. "Where is everyone?"

Ash had shoveled a spoonful of stew into his mouth but watched Butch and Sundance for an answer as he chewed.

Sundance shrugged. "Gone. I'm not sure where Curry went. I think Will went to Laramie, and Flat Nose and his brothers might've gone to Cheyenne. Took their share of the take and hightailed it."

Butch nodded. "You boys did good from what I hear. Followed the plan exactly. Sent the second train all the hell the way back to Cheyenne."

"Yes, sir. We did." Ash grinned. "Wasn't hard either."

Grant dipped a piece of his bread into his bowl. "There was a second explosion. We heard it, and we could see smoke. What happened?"

Butch grinned. "Well, sir, that there is a funny story. See, the man guarding the money in the second car—what was his name, Sundance?"

"Charles Wood-something."

Butch nodded. "That was it! Woodcock, you said. I thought it was a hoot of a name. Anyway, this Charles refused to open the express car. Our boys had already been through the mail car and didn't find squat. They knew the money had to be in there, 'specially when Charlie-boy wouldn't open the door. So, they blew it open. Knocked poor Charles off his feet like a leaf from a tree."

Butch laughed again, and even Sundance cracked a smile.

Grant urged Butch to tell the rest of the story. "We heard four explosions. That's only three."

Butch held up a hand. "Yup, I can count, son. The fourth is the killer of this story. The boys found the safe in express car—guess that's why Charles was so reluctant to open the door—but it was locked, and Charles was too addled by the explosion to open it, even if he knew the combination.

"What to do? Why, blow the safe, of course!" Butch was still laughing, tears actually forming in his eyes. "But the idiots used too much dynamite! They blew the safe, sure, but they also blew the money sky high!" He slapped his knee, guffawing. "Oh, I would've given my left nut to be there, to see Kid and Curry and the rest scrambling around snatching money out of the air and up from the ground."

Sundance snorted. "Sounds funnier than it was."

"Aw, I bet it was purely comical." Humor gleamed in Butch's eyes, even as his cackles finally faded to snickers. He wiped his eyes with the back of his hand. "They done good though. Got fifty thousand."

"Wow! That's a lot of money." It didn't sound like much to Grant, but he knew fifty thousand in 1899 would probably be well over a million dollars in his own time.

"Sure is. We're rich, boys!" He pulled out two stacks of

bills, each tied with a length of brown twine. "Here's your split. Ain't what the rest of the gang got—they took the real risk—but it's enough to get you both started off somewhere, if that's what you please."

"Or to get yourselves a month-long drunk and a passel of women," Sundance put in.

Grant stared at the money, then haltingly reached for his stack. Ash did the same. "Um, wow. Thanks, Butch."

"You earned it. Sundance said you done good. Sent the second train back the way it came."

Ash nodded. "Yeah. The engineer said he was going to backtrack all the way to Cheyenne."

"Is he, now? Ain't that something." Butch stood up and stretched. "Well, we was waiting for you two to get back. Us three are riding out to Laramie, then probably on to Cheyenne. After we drink the city dry, we may head east. Etta's got an itch to see New York City."

Grant's eyes flashed open. "Wow, New York? It's a huge city." He suddenly realized what he'd said. As far as Butch knew, he'd never been farther than Nebraska. "Or so I've heard."

Butch grinned. "I hear they have buildings so high you can't hardly see the tops, and a genuine menagerie in a park, right in the middle of it."

Etta collected Butch and Sundance's mugs and rinsed them in a bucket of water. "They have fancy restaurants out there too. Better even than Cheyenne. And women in lace and expensive hats have afternoon tea and eat elegant little sandwiches."

Sundance smiled at her. "And you'll have the best hat we can buy on Fifth Avenue and drink tea until you slosh."

Grant bit back a smile that Sundance would not have appreciated had he let it loose, but it was obvious how much

Sundance loved Etta. Ash's elbow digging into his side told him Ash thought it was adorable too.

Butch stood and reached for his hat, while Etta and Sundance readied themselves to leave as well. "You boys are welcome to tag along with us, if you want."

Ash shook his head. "Oh, thanks, Butch. We'd love to, but we, uh..."

Grant finished Ash's sentence. "We'd been wanting to see California. Heard there's lots of gold out there. Maybe go to San Francisco."

Butch smiled. "Well, then, good luck to you. Keep the wind at your backs, boys."

Panic tickled Grant's belly. He realized Butch didn't plan to return to Hole in the Wall, at least not for a while. What if he took his prized gun with him?

"You two can stay here for a spell if you want. Rest up. There's still beef in the smokehouse. We're going to set the cows free. No sense in keeping them here—nobody's going to be around to milk and feed them." Butch stuck his hand out for a shake. "Been a pleasure riding with you boys."

Grant shook Butch's hand, and then Ash took a turn. "Thanks, Butch. For everything."

Butch winked at them, then walked outside. Sundance and Etta said their farewells and followed Butch. Not long after, Grant and Ash stood on the cabin's porch and watched the three outlaws ride off.

They remained on the porch until Butch, Sundance, and Etta's horses disappeared over the edge of the high bluff, then returned to the cabin. It was a little sad. They both liked Butch a lot. He'd been really good to them, like a big brother. Grant knew he and Ash were going to miss him. And while Sundance and Etta had been more standoffish, neither had done anything to hurt or make Grant and Ash's life any more difficult. Grant wished them all well.

"What if it's not here? What if he took it with him?" Ash sounded near panic and brought Grant out of his thoughts. "Maybe we should've gone with them. If we leave now, we can catch up."

"We need to look in the cabin first, before we panic." Grant put a steadying hand on Ash's arm. "We know where they're going. Laramie, then Cheyenne. Butch wasn't sure they were going on to New York. Maybe he figures he'll be back to Hole in the Wall to get it first. If not, we can catch up to them in Laramie or Cheyenne if we need to."

Ash sucked in a deep breath and nodded. "Okay." He looked dejected as he walked back inside the cabin. "He had it hidden under the bed. But I bet it's gone. He liked it too much to leave it behind."

"I know, but we might as well look while we're here. Do you really want to jump on our horses and ride to catch up with them only to find out he left it behind?"

"I guess you're right. But I still say he took it with him."

They hurried to the back of the cabin and dropped to their knees next to the bed.

"Please, please, please," Ash whispered. It sounded like a prayer, like he was hoping against hope.

Grant totally understood Ash's desperation. He wanted to go home too. He was tired of the wild Wild West. Tired of the dust, the food, the heat. His butt was sure as hell tired of riding a horse. He wanted hot and cold running water again. Actual toilets. Fast food. The internet. And about a million other things he knew he tended to take for granted.

Ash bent lower, pressing his cheek to the worn floorboards while he swept his arm under the bed. Suddenly, a broad smile lit his face, and a moment later, he dragged out a metal box. *The* metal box, the one Butch kept his gun in.

But was the Colt still in the box, or had Butch taken it with him?

Grant and Ash exchanged a nervous look. "Go on," Grant said. "Open it."

Ash bit his lip and lifted the lid.

Inside was the Colt .45 and a handwritten note. Grant picked it up and read it aloud.

This is for you, boys. I know you greatly admired it, and I want you to have it. You remind me a lot of myself as a lad. I hope you have as much luck with it as I did. Your Friend, Butch Cassidy.

Ash let out a whoop that made Grant's ears ring. "We got it! We can go home!"

Grant laughed. "Yes! Man, Butch was a great guy, even if he was an outlaw! Are you ready to go?"

"Do you really even have to ask?"

Together, they reached into the box and touched the gun.

The world spun, thunder rolled inside the cabin, and Merlin's magic whisked them away.

EPILOGUE

Ash sat up, feeling woozy as he always did when he came back from a field trip to another time. He realized he was in Merlin's history classroom, but it took a few more minutes for his mind to fully clear. When it did, the first thing he looked for was Grant, who was sitting nearby, also on the floor. The second was the Colt, which was nowhere in sight.

"Where's the gun? What happened to it?" He patted his pockets, then swept his hands across the floor, looking frantically around for it. "Do you have it?"

Grant blinked at him, then understanding seemed to dawn in his eyes. He repeated Ash's actions, checking his own pockets. "Oh! No, I don't have it. I don't know what happened to it!"

"Did we lose it? We've never lost an artifact on the way home before." The last thing he wanted was for Merlin to send them back to 1899 to get the Colt *again*. He wanted a hot bath and a meal, preferably a thick burger and a tall, frosty milkshake.

"Gentlemen, take a breath. You did not lose the Colt,

although I am sure if *anyone* could find a way to lose the artifact they'd just retrieved during the short jaunt home from the past, it would be you two. I have the weapon."

They both looked up at the sound of Merlin's voice. He was seated at his desk at the head of the classroom. His piercing blue eyes stared at them from under his familiar bushy white eyebrows. "You certainly didn't think I would leave a weapon in the hands of two students, do you?"

"Why, Mr. Ambrosius? We used guns when we were in 1899, and neither of us managed to shoot ourselves or anyone else." Ash felt a little put off. Merlin thought they were mature enough to handle a weapon in 1899 but not in their own time? It didn't make sense.

Merlin pinned Ash with an icy blue glare. "In the past, you are required to behave as one your age would in that specific time. When you are here, you will behave according to the laws governing this time. No weapons are allowed at the Stanton School for Boys. Even this one, an unloaded antique of great value, is to be kept in my office, locked in a gun safe. In this time, children do not fire weapons, and with good reason. There have been and, sadly, continue to be, far too many tragedies involving firearms."

"Yet you sent two kids back in time to get this one." Grant cringed as if he feared his mouth had just earned him a lightning bolt up his butt, but surprisingly, nothing happened.

Instead, Merlin sighed. "I admit, I was deeply torn while making the decision. Of all the artifacts you destroyed, I was most hesitant to send you back to retrieve this one."

"Then why did you?" Grant asked, but Ash was just as curious.

"I knew Butch Cassidy, although an outlaw, was an honorable man with a sense of compassion. In his entire career, he never killed anyone. The men he rode with did, but he did not. He was also generous and known to be kind. I felt he would protect you, and it seems, I was correct." He paused, then continued. "You've also shown me on your previous trips to the past that you can be trusted and are resourceful when necessary. Quick to adapt."

Ash looked at Grant, and they both grinned. It was the first time Merlin had ever complimented them. They felt like they'd just scored an A on a test they'd dreaded for months.

Merlin cleared his throat, and his former, irascible personality emerged once again. "At least, you've managed not to kill yourselves in the past. Not yet, anyway. You should not become complacent. You are still in a great deal of trouble. You have many more objects to retrieve before you finish making restitution for the trouble you've caused me." He sniffed and looked down his long, narrow nose at them. "I still highly question your intelligence and ability to finish the year without being thrown out on your ears."

Now that was the Merlin they knew. Ash bit back a smile. "Mr. Ambrosius, what happened to Butch and Sundance and Etta? Did they ever make it to New York?"

Merlin looked at the Colt he held, turning it over in his hands. He waggled the fingers of one hand over it and mumbled a few words in a language neither Ash nor Grant understood. The gun disappeared, probably sent to wherever Merlin was storing his artifacts these days. Then he tented his fingers, rested his bearded chin on them, and closed his eyes. "There was a great manhunt for the Wild Bunch after the train robbery, but those three were never caught. They went to New York—by train, ironically—and by all reports, had a wonderful time. After New York, they went to South America. It was Butch's idea, thinking no one was looking for them there. They wanted to become respectable, put their outlaw days behind them.

"For a while, they succeeded. They bought land, intending to be farmers. It seems old habits die hard though.

Too soon, Butch and Sundance returned to their outlaw ways."

Ash and Grant watched Merlin in rapt attention, caught up in the tale of Butch and Sundance's last days. "What happened to them then?"

"No one knows what happened to Etta. She left South America alone and returned to the United States, to San Francisco. Then she simply disappeared. Some claim she became a schoolteacher, which was her profession before she took up with the Wild Bunch. Others claim she earned her living by more nefarious methods, as a prostitute. I prefer to think she settled somewhere and lived out her life peacefully."

Ash smiled, a little sadly. "I hope that's what happened to her too. She was a nice lady. I mean, not especially friendly, but she wasn't mean, and she made a great stew."

Merlin rolled his eyes. "Is your barometer of human character always your stomach?" He waved a hand at Ash as if dismissing him and continued the story. "What happened to Butch and Sundance is a bit of a mystery as well. They returned to being outlaws, as I've said. One day, they robbed the payroll of a silver mine in southern Bolivia. It was a mistake. The owner of a boardinghouse they stopped at saw a mule they had in their possession. The mule was branded as belonging to the mine. He alerted the authorities, who cornered Butch and Sundance in the house. There was a standoff, and according to Bolivian records, Butch and Sundance committed suicide rather than be captured by the Bolivian soldiers."

Grant sat up on his knees. "I don't believe it!"

Ash agreed. "Neither do I. Butch wouldn't take the chicken's way out. He was an outlaw, but he was brave."

Grant nodded. "Yeah. And he was wicked smart. He would've thought of a way to get out of there. And if he robbed a mine, he would've had a plan worked out ahead of time."

Merlin held up a hand again, but Ash could see a tiny smile hitching Merlin's lips under his beard. "That is the official story, but there have always been rumors, stories told for generations that claim Butch, at least, did not die in Bolivia but made it back to the United States. Cassidy's own family claimed he returned to Circleville, his childhood home. Others say he went to Baggs, Wyoming, somewhere the Wild Bunch often spent time. In any case, it is all conjecture. There is no proof he and Sundance died in Bolivia, just as there is no evidence Cassidy returned to North America. Their ends remain a mystery."

"I think he made it home again." Ash really wanted it to be true. He'd liked Butch. He wanted to think Butch got a happily ever after.

Merlin sighed. "I think, perhaps, we'll never know the truth. In any case, his Colt .45 is once again safe and where it belongs—under lock and key. Now, I believe it's time for supper. You'd best hurry before the cafeteria runs out of fish sticks or whatever other culinary atrocity they're serving today. And don't forget—there'll be a test on Monday morning regarding World War II, in particular the Battle of Midway. I expect you to be prepared."

And with that final snippy reminder, Merlin disappeared.

Ash sighed heavily. "A test. You'd think he'd cut us a break, considering we just got back. My butt still hurts from all the riding we did."

"Merlin? Give us a break?" Grant reached out and felt Ash's forehead. "Are you sick or just crazy?"

"I feel okay, so I guess I'm just nuts."

Grant laughed, and Ash had to admit it was a great sound. He was suddenly very happy to be home. He was also ravenous. "Come on. I'm so hungry even fish sticks are sounding good to me."

He stood and reached for Grant's hand, then helped Grant up from the floor. Grant surprised him by popping to his feet quickly and ducking in to steal a kiss.

Not that Ash minded. Not one bit.

Grant pulled away and started for the classroom door, but Ash caught his hand and pulled him back.

"You know, there's something to be said for repeating history," Ash said, just before drawing Grant into another much longer, deeper kiss.

The fish sticks, Ash thought, *canA wait.*

www.ingramcontent.com/pod-product-compliance
Lightning Source LLC
Chambersburg PA
CBHW060942180626
46817CB00004B/1676